A Suitable

IBSN 978-0-9555427-1-8

Best regards and hope the
Drones entertain

Bidie Burwell .

Dedication

This book is dedicated to Roy, my husband, love of my life, soul mate, best friend and greatest critic (no matter how harshly he has judged my writing at times ouch). His encouragement has been constant .Like me he has his faults and can be a right pain in the posterior ha ha, but I would not change one thing about him.

To the reader I sincerely hope that you enjoy some if not all the stories in this collection. Writing them has been a great adventure for me and I have loved every minute.

Contents

The house of my dreams featured in a period television drama. The moment I laid eyes on the sparkling white Art Deco mansion, its architectural beauty took my breath away. The building had a bowed frontage. The curved double front doors were inlaid with panels of stained glass revealing peacocks with glistening plumage in bright jewel colours of green, blue and gold. The curvature of the front porch and steel framed circular windows were reminiscent of an ocean going liner of the 1930s.

Out of the blue one Monday morning, a white envelope slid through the letterbox and landed silently on the monochrome tiled hall floor. It didn't occur to me then that this seemingly ordinary letter would change the course of my life. The handwritten envelope was hastily shoved into my pocket before I left the house. My thoughts were fully concentrated on the working day ahead.

At 5.30pm I returned to my empty two bedroomed Victorian terraced home. Paul my husband, was abroad working on a twelve month engineering contract. As I took off my coat the envelope slipped from my pocket. My first course of action was to make a pot of tea; before settling down at the kitchen table. I then carefully slid   the sharp edge of a knife blade along the fold at the top of the envelope. To my amazement the letter was a legal document, posted to me from a local branch

of Solicitors, named Robbins and Steel.

While reading the contents of the letter my eyes widened both in surprise and pure delight; on discovering I was named as beneficiary in a will. I was advised to arrange an appointment with Mr Steel, as soon as possible. The name of the benefactor was not mentioned in the letter, which set my curiosity running wild.

Later on, that same evening Paul phoned. We looked forward to our weekly conversations. We also kept in touch by email and letters, which were filled with details about our daily lives. He was due to come home in a couple of months for ten days leave. We both looked forward so much to spending some time together. I excitedly told him about the Solicitors letter, before reading the contents of it over the phone. He immediately registered his suspicion. His voice when he spoke, was heavy with concern.

'Sarah! Crazy as it sounds. I have a really bad feeling about this. Why would a total stranger make you a beneficiary of their will? It just doesn't make any sense to me. Please, promise me that you will be cautious, don't make any rash decisions. I love you so much!'

'You worry too much Paul. Knowing my luck it will turn out to be a request to feed someone's cat for the duration. You are all too familiar with my fear of cats. The constant sounds of purring and meowing really creeps me out. I love you too! I'm counting the days, hours, and minutes until you come home. You don't have to worry about me. I will be phoning Mr Steel to arrange an appointment. Be assured I will listen avidly to what he has to tell me, before carefully considering whether to accept the legacy, whatever that might turn out to be!'

We talked for an hour, then reluctantly bid each other goodnight. After the phone conversation had ended I poured myself a glass of wine. The long busy day coupled with the excitement of the letter, the phone call, and now the wine soon took its toll. My eyelids felt much too heavy to stay open. I decided to have an early night. The last task of the day was to check the doors and window locks. I had never quite come to terms with my fear of the darkness. The nightly ritual of locking up the house had to be carried out meticulously. I would not be able to rest until secure in the knowledge that my home was safe and sound.

Almost immediately I drifted along the misty realm of sleep, slipping through the veil of subconscious into a dream which was difficult to distinguish from reality. I found myself walking down a long winding lane. The glow of warm sunlight shining down on my face felt glorious. At the very end of the lane stood a long brick wall with a set of wide intricately detailed wrought iron gates at the centre. The art deco style design on each gate was that of a ship sailing over the waves.

As I approached the gates, they began to swing inwards. It seemed an age until the scene beyond came into full view. In amazement I caught my breath at the sight revealed before me, it truly was awesome in its magnificence. Through the ever widening gap in the gates, I glimpsed a long sweeping drive leading towards a stunning white mansion. I remembered in vivid detail that television drama seen so long ago. The building appeared to be identical in design from where I was standing.

I had the impression the place was deserted. An eerie silence hung over the estate, which was unnerving to say the least. There was no sound whatsoever, even the air around me seemed to be inexplicably still. Fleetingly I wondered if this really were a dream. It seemed much too vivid in clarity and detail, to be anything other than reality. Why was no-one to be seen? There had to be at least one person around here, if only to operate the control panel for the gates.

The lawns before me were a lush shade of green. The grass was cut precisely into uniform blades of exact length. The flower beds were perfectly co-ordinated, each bloom a pastel shade of pink or blue. It was then I noticed the place was not deserted. On the path close to the house were two peacocks strutting regally along, proudly displaying their plumage.

Realisation dawned with a shock, that this was private property. The last thing I needed was to be caught trespassing. A wave of fear overcame me causing a sudden urge to retreat. With mounting horror I found my body was no longer under my control. Against my will I was being propelled at great speed towards the mansion. The awareness that someone lurked inside waiting, paralysed me with fear.   Revulsion churned my insides at the thought of meeting whoever that might be. I dreaded to think what would happen if I set eyes on the stranger lying in wait.

The urge to flee helped me regain control of my legs. I was determined to escape this place and reach safety beyond the gates. As I turned my back on the mansion another wave of fear settled heavily across my shoulders holding me rigid. The gates at the end of the drive were swinging shut, the gap folding much quicker than when they opened. The thought of being trapped inside set the adrenalin pumping, my legs regained control and started to push me forward.

'Come on Sarah keep calm and run. Get away from this place!'

It shocked me to hear the terror in my voice. I breathed in deeply, exhaling very slowly a couple of times. Better keep control and walk to the gates, any sudden movement may! May what? Alert the guards; dogs; something much, much worse!

I willed myself to keep moving forward and banish the mounting terror. That resolve lasted but seconds. The sensation of ice forming across the surface of a lake crept slowly along my spine. Tiny frozen bolts of shock danced across my scalp causing my hair to stand on end. Something evil was lurking inside the mansion. I had no wish to discover what that might be. On the wide screen inside my head a message flashed up. The words were clear, run, run for your life!

Hysteria took hold for a split second before another rush of adrenalin gave me the strength needed to escape. My legs nearly took flight as I ran with great speed towards the swinging gates. I ran as if my very life were at stake. To my great relief the gap was just about wide enough for me to slip through. I reached the safety of the lane just as the gates shut behind me like a pair of snapping jaws, failing to catch their prey. I kept on running until the safety of the main road was reached.

I awoke from that nightmare gasping for breath, a cold dark mantle of fear draped across my shoulders chilling me to the bone. For the remainder of the night I stayed awake. Every light in the house was switched on, illumination extinguishing all darkness and shadows.

How I longed to not be alone. I had no close family members, just a few distant relatives who lived hundreds of miles away. My neighbours were virtually strangers. We were on nodding terms only. My closest friend would never understand my abject fear of the dark. We had known each other for years but some things were best left unspoken. Apart from Paul there was no-one I trusted enough to confide in.

For most of the next day until work finished at 4.30pm there was little or no time to dwell on the events of the previous night. At 5pm precisely I stepped through the main door and into the reception area of Robbins and Steel .The smartly dressed young receptionist smiled brightly as I introduced myself, she asked me to take a seat for a moment. Seconds later I was escorted into the office of Mr Steel. It was a large room the main desk looked neat and tidy, but the spare one was piled high with files and documents. Mr Steel greeted me with a firm handshake. He looked to be in his mid-40s. His brown eyes beheld a warmth and sincerity. I noted his hair was almost black and cut into a neat short style. He wore a dark grey suit and I noticed his black leather brogues were highly polished. It was reassuring in a way to see that this man took great pride in his appearance. Someone so meticulous had to be trustworthy.

'Good afternoon Mrs Hart. You must be curious regarding the identity of your benefactor. Is the name George Price familiar to you?'

'I don't know anyone of that name.'

'Mr Price came to this office and asked me to transcribe his (Last Will and Testament) ten years ago. At that time he presented me with a letter to be passed on to you in the event of his death. Having handed over the letter I was to await your decision, before proceeding to the next stage.'

'I confess to being curious but also more than a little apprehensive. How could Mr Price know of me, when I've no recollection of ever having met him?'

'As to that question I have no answer. Hopefully all will be revealed in the contents of this envelope.'

'Thanks Mr Steel, I will contact you as soon as I've reached a decision.'

I walked the long route home and the fresh air and exercise helped me to think with clarity. Paul's voice urging me to be cautious kept repeating inside my head like a mantra.

It was quite a fascinating thought as to how my benefactor even knew who I was, let alone why he wished to bequeath a legacy. It was indeed a real life mystery.

I soon arrived home, filled the teapot and settled at my kitchen table turning the letter over and over in my hands many times while my brain worked over time. Briefly I thought about ripping it to shreds and throwing the pieces in the bin. But the decision was made when my curiosity, at first minimal, slowly burned with intensity. I still couldn't dismiss a sense of foreboding, yet the need to discover the contents banished all dark thoughts to the back of my mind. I literally tore open the envelope in a fever of excitement. With trembling fingers I pulled out the letter, unfolded the creases and avidly read those few brief lines of sweeping black Italic script.

Seawinds

Ocean Lane

Pendleton

Dear Mrs Hart,

Your intervention on that most fateful day so many years ago, led directly to the extension my life. For that very reason it is now my decision that you should be suitably rewarded.

Mr Steel is in possession of a letter containing all the details. If you have any doubts then please dispel them immediately.

Trust me when I say, you are most deserving of this legacy.

Yours sincerely

George Price

The penny dropped instantly as a memory stirred inside my brain. Ten years previously I had been employed in the city centre and commuted each day by rail. It was while waiting at the station one evening that the incident occurred. I glanced across the platform and noticed a man standing so dangerously close to the edge of the platform he was in danger of falling on to the tracks. Instinctively I rushed over and pulled him back to safety before the train rolled in and ground to a halt. I never spoke to him, just walked away and boarded the train without a backward glance. I settled into a seat near the window. Instinctively I knew someone was watching me. I glanced at the platform to find that same man staring so intently as if to mentally imprint the memory of my face on to his mind. I never told anyone about the incident and all memory of it was forgotten until now.

The next day I found myself seated once again in the office of Mr Steel. I carefully read the contents of the letter he handed over to me before deciding there and then to accept the legacy. Mr Steel made a phone call and thirty minutes later a young man entered the office dressed in the dark grey uniform of a chauffeur. He shook my hand saying.

'Pleased to meet you Mrs Hart. My name is Roberts. I've been instructed to drive you directly to Seawinds.'

Seated in the back of the luxurious Silver Bentley was at first a wonderful experience. Who hasn't dreamed of being chauffeur driven in a car of such opulence? That feeling of extravagance in the plush surroundings of the limousine did not last long however.

As the Bentley headed out of town it struck me that something was not quite right. Roberts had remained eerily silent since he closed the door behind me, as I settled into the luxurious interior at the rear of the car. When I asked the whereabouts of Seawinds; he stared directly at the road ahead as if he hadn't heard the question.

All too soon the car turned off the main road and manoeuvred expertly along the narrow winding country lane. Tremors of fear shivered along the length of my spine as I recognised the familiarity of the surroundings. Oh no! I screamed silently inside, this couldn't be happening! I must be still dreaming. I was desperate to escape. This was the lane I had walked along in my nightmare. Almost immediately the long brick wall and iron gates were visible straight ahead. The cold tentacles of fear reached out and caught me in a chilling embrace.

I tried to open a door but they were both locked, the window buttons had been removed. There was no escape, I mentally planned to make a run for it on arrival at the destination. The gates slowly swung inwards to reveal the familiar dream scene beyond. The neatly clipped lawns, sweeping drive, peacocks and large white mansion were no longer a dream but stark reality. Whatever the legacy contained, I now wanted none of it! The car came to an abrupt stop in front of the house. Roberts opened both the drivers and passenger door and escorted me towards the main entrance, all the while holding my arm in a vice like grip.

The front doors were opened as soon as we reached the entrance. An exceptionally tall, stern featured woman, dressed head to toe in black invited me into the hall. She held out her arms in a theatrical flourish and drew me inside, much as a spider catching a fly. In total silence she walked ahead of me down the long corridor, leading me ever further inside the main body of the beautiful house.

Before too long she came to a standstill outside white louvered double doors, the style of which also reminded me of the interior of a ship. She pushed them open and I was ushered into an elegant sitting room, furnished and decorated in the art deco style to match the exterior. A circular white coffee table had been set for afternoon tea, complete with bone china service and a matching cake stand. There was an array of sandwiches without crusts cut into bite sized triangles, plus a selection of cakes and scones with tiny dishes of butter, clotted cream and a selection of flavoured jams. As soon as I was settled into an arm chair she poured the tea and handed me a cup.

'My name is Miss Rainbird, I'm housekeeper of the Seawinds Estate. I have lived in and run this house for the late Mr Price for more years than even I can remember. Please do drink your tea Mrs Hart. Mr Price left specific instructions, the first of which; that I was to provide you with these refreshments. He wanted to be sure you were given a cup of tea, before I handed over the letter.'

Her voice was a revelation, she spoke in a soothing mellow tone, so dissimilar to how I imagined she would sound, given her appearance. After savouring the aroma I cautiously lifted the cup to my lips and relished that first sip of the hot strong tea, enjoying the flavour as well as admiring the delicate, almost transparent china it was served in. Almost immediately relief began to flow through me like the calming waters of a flowing stream. My body began to loosen the tension of knotted muscles and jangled nerves. It had been such a waste of energy to be so fearful and suspicious. Everything was going to be alright now, I was certain of that. It was totally irrational on my part to have been so worried. My nerves were soothingly calm, shoulders slumped at ease.

I glanced across the table to find Miss Rainbird staring at me with a manner of intense concentration. For a moment I thought the gleam in her eyes was full of malice, but just as quickly her eyelids dropped like a blind and when she opened them a split second later there was no hint of it. The corners of her mouth lifted into what appeared to be a genuine smile as she handed me the letter. I gazed at the envelope edged in black and thought how old fashioned it seemed in this day and age. Then suddenly remembering letters of bereavement, were once delivered in black bordered envelopes; a shudder reverberated along my spine. I picked up the silver letter opener from the tray, then slid the sharp blade along the edge of the envelope. I took out the single sheet of paper. As I read the words; my blood ran ice cold through my veins as the horror of my situation became apparent.

Dear Mrs Hart,

If you are reading this letter my last instructions have been carried out successfully. The day you decided to interfere with my plan to commit suicide, I swore that sometime in the future you would be suitably rewarded for that course of action.

I had been diagnosed as having Motor Neurone Disease that very day. The horror of knowing what was to come seemed intolerable. It was for that reason I decided to put an end to my life.

After that first attempt there was no other opportunity left for me to try again. The disease progressed with a vengeance almost immediately.

P.S. Now you are facing the consequences of your actions. The tea is poisoned by the way.

Maybe I will see you on the other side ha ha!

Bon Voyage
George Price

I more or less frog marched him to our local pub, ordered five pints for him then asked him outright.

'Who are you?'

He was already in shock from me dragging him out of the house; steering him into the pub; telling him to sit down when we got there, marching swiftly to the bar and ordering not one but five pints of his favourite bitter. I had never once took him to the pub before. Never was I the one to go to the bar and order the drinks, and definitely never the one to actually pay for the rounds. Eddie always bought the drinks while I found us a table.

I felt a bit awkward standing at the bar among the mainly male customers. Victor the friendly young Ukrainian bar manager came right over.

'Good evening, where is your husband tonight?'

I pointed to a table close to the window and he gave me a quizzical glance, eyebrows raised then smiled.

'What can I get for you?'

I ordered five pints of Pedigree best bitter.

'I will bring them to the table they are too heavy for you to carry.'

I thanked him, paid for the round and walked over to the table. Eddie looked shocked when Victor brought the laden tray of drinks over and placed them in a row in front of him. I hadn't ordered anything for myself. There was a heavy cloying silence after I'd asked him the question! What seemed like hours, but was in fact maybe a minute; two at the most. Eddie stared at me as if I were a complete stranger.

'Christ what the hell are you playing at? Why have you bought five pints for goodness sake? You know my limit is four pints over an entire evening out, not in one round? Four pints and I go home sober, five and the arrow tips over the scale to downright sozzled. What's that supposed to mean, who are you? Stop mucking me about!'

I stared back at him just as intently. Silence hung in the air between us like a great dark vulture getting ready to devour a corpse. I had a vision of the creature; ugly long neck, black wings, cold eyes gleaming. I shuddered. Eddie brought me back to the present.

'I'm not going to drink any of these pints unless you have a drink with me, so what's it to be?'

'I'll have half a lager please.'

'How about a glass of Chardonnay instead?'

'Okay then but just a small one thanks.'

He went to the bar and my thoughts drifted back to the holiday in Cyprus just a few weeks ago. Everything changed after visiting the Bath of Aphrodite; it was the 8th day of our ten day holiday. Eddie had hired a car so we could explore the sights of Pathos. We both took a great deal of interest in history and archaeology. This was the perfect place to see so many places of historical significance!

From the very first day, we had eagerly set off out early each morning. We wanted to see as much as possible every single day, knowing full well that time has a habit of speeding up during the holidays. So far we had visited the Adonis Baths, Acropolis and Odeon, the Agios Georgios Basilica and the Fountains of Pegeia. The Tombs of the Kings and the Temple of Aphrodite had been so wonderful to behold. It was very quiet being February and could be quite cool, but with me being ever the optimist I had only packed summer clothes. Eddie had kindly lent me his spare fleece every day, even though he had warned me it would not be that hot, he didn't want me to get cold. He was always so thoughtful. The cold breezes could not dampen my enthusiasm or the sheer joy, of walking around sites that people from thousands of years ago had tread their way on these same paths. We managed to get lost a couple of times but even then made light of the situation even though six times we drove up into the hills and on our return came to the same crossroads where all direction posts North, South, East and West pointed to the same destination, Pathos!

We drove around for goodness knows how many hours before finding our way back to the hotel. Some of the residents, well in fact 90% of them were elderly and had booked in for three months, paying the same as we did for 10 days. Good on them we thought. They were on the whole a lively bunch. Every morning at 8 o'clock on the dot a crowd of pensioners gathered beneath our balcony at the pools edge, and performed a set of none too vigorous exercise routines to Max Bygraves songs. We would laugh about it, but not at the men and women just the fact that all the bending and waving of arms too, 'you need hands', seemed really comical for some reason.

Each evening we enjoyed our meal accompanied by locally brewed beers or wine. We always made our plans for the next days' trip during the evening. There were several Hotels close by, so it was great to walk off the meal and take a look at whichever entertainments were on offer each evening. Most evenings there would be a choice of several cabaret shows to watch. All in all we were having a really fantastic time. It saddens me to remember the complete change that come over Eddie that fateful day. Now when I thought about it the scene played out in my mind as if watching a clip of the main movie.

The cool breeze had calmed down and it felt a little warmer on that day. The Baths of Aphrodite like all the other ancient sites were steeped in legend. The main attraction supposedly was the fact that the cool green waters would rejuvenate anyone who cared to bathe in the pool. I can't stand the cold so there was no chance of me taking a dip. I did manage to submerge my hands and cup the water in my palms before splashing the droplets on to my face. A little of the water managed to slide down my throat and I coughed like crazy until Eddie patted my back and the foul tasting water rose up through my throat and gushed forward. It was not a nice experience but my recovery was swift. Eddie who is a fantastic swimmer decided to take a dip in the pool even though neither of us had a towel.

For some inexplicable reason I tried to persuade him not to enter the water. He laughed and said.

'I will soon dry out, what's the problem? You worry too much!'

With that he stripped to his birthday suit and dived into the deep waters of the pool. He was completely submerged and I held my breath waiting for him to break through the surface of the water and laugh at me for my silly fears. The seconds ticked by 10, 20, 30, 40, 50, a minute. I was full of concern and shouted.

'Come on out you are scaring me, this isn't funny, please....'

The sentence trailed off and an eerie silence surrounded me on all sides. Time seemed to literally come to a stop. I glanced at my wrist watch and the hour, minute and second hands had frozen. For a second or two I gasped for breath as a cold numbness started to freeze my feet; it moved up through my ankles, calves, knees, and throughout my torso. I could not move, my body was becoming paralysed little by little until the numbness reached my chest. I felt the pressure squeezing my lungs and the fight or flight reaction set in. I closed my eyes and visualised my inner spirit breaking the invisible bonds that would trap my body and hold me prisoner against my will. A glimmer of warmth flickered inside my chest like a candle spluttering in the draft from an open window. The glimmer became a flickering flame of bright yellow with a core of deep crimson. The heat spread along my veins and muscles like a power surge. I was in control once again. My watch had started ticking, the birds sang and the insects burst forth with their own unique chorus.

A slight breeze moved through the branches, they shook a little, flower petals dropped to the ground like confetti being thrown at a wedding. The breeze grew stronger and the branches shook vigorously in a menacing manner. Since my watch hands froze I had not given Eddie a thought. Now the iron fist grabbed my insides and terror filled me like poisonous venom.

'Eddie where are you, please comeback....'

The tears burst forth and flowed fast with fury down my cheeks. I ran to the waters' edge and looked into the pool my tears falling on to the surface mingling with the cold green liquid. Just then Eddie burst through the water and swam towards me at a fast pace. He emerged from the pool and shook himself, as a dog might to be rid of excess water. He dressed quickly and then seemed to notice me. He stared at me as if I were a stranger, then noticed the tears and distress, but instead of showing any concern, he turned away, saying.

'Right then we better get back to the hotel I need a shower.'

On the journey back it was as if his mind was somewhere else, and when I tried to speak he cut me off with a terse.

'Look I'm tired so I don't want to hear whatever it is you have to say. Give it a rest for a change.'

His facial features seemed to belong to a stranger. All warmth had evaporated. He glanced at me quickly, eyes cold like a serpent, contempt etched in the grim set of his lips. He dismissed me with a curt nod and concentrated on the road ahead. He never spoke a single word on the way back to the hotel. The rest of the holiday was endured not enjoyed. The closeness, the fun and the laughter had disappeared that day and Eddie was no longer the man I knew and had loved for so many years.

Since we had returned home he had been like a total stranger. He never smiled anymore, and seemed to have forgotten the meaning of the word laughter. He turned away from me each time I tried to show any affection. Every time I attempted to talk to him he ignored me and walked away.

Everything changed last night with my decision to get to the root of the problem. I was determined life could not carry on in this way. Eddie had not touched a drop of alcohol since the swim in Aphrodite's Bath. That was it! Everything clicked into place, the cool green waters of the pool had changed him somehow. Occasionally when I glanced at him, his expression seemed to shift as if a veil had descended mask like, hiding his true features. I realised last night that Eddie may still be my husband in body; but in heart, soul and mind he had somehow been possessed by something or someone, malevolent! That was when I decided to get him drunk and lower his defences, or at least have a good try. I loved my husband and wanted him back.

Eddie returned from the bar carrying a bottle of wine and a large glass. So I thought, he was on to me, whoever the hell he was! I thanked him and poured half a glass of the Chardonnay. I urged him pick to up a pint and clinked my glass to his saying.

'Cheers,' in as pleasant a voice as I could possibly manage.

'Chris what did you mean, when you asked, who are you?'

I decided to change my tactics.

'Oh Eddie, I wasn't being serious love. But admit it, I got you going there for a minute!'

I laughed and sipped the wine, nudging Eddie and pointing to his first glass of beer. He looked at the pints and something strange happened. His eyes turned from their usual green to a shade of amber like those of a tiger. Just as quickly they turned back to green. He just stared at me as if expecting a reaction. I acted normally so as not to arouse his suspicion. He sipped at the first pint in a wary manner at first, then started to gulp it down and in seconds the glass was empty. Victor had left the bar to collect glasses and came over to our table to retrieve Eddies'.

'You must be very thirsty tonight.' He smiled at Eddie.

The second glass disappeared just as quickly as the first, then the third pint was drunk with equal speed. Eddie was oblivious to everything but the pints of Pedigree bitter. As he picked up the fourth pint, his hand started to shake as if being controlled by some invisible force. Every time he tried to raise the glass it would not move from the table. His eyes changed rapidly from green to amber, then returned to green again, just like the sequence of traffic lights but a speeded up version. His head started to shake violently and fear caught me in its grip. The rapid change going on inside Eddie held me both fascinated and horrified at the same time.

Now his body seemed to be in the throes of some violent struggle, yet he still tried in vain to hold on to the glass and raise it to his lips. An eerie sound, guttural almost demonic escaped from the depths of his throat. He stared at me and I could see in his eyes the pleading for my intervention. I picked up the 5th pint glass with both hands and held it to his lips forcing his mouth open. His head tilted back and the beer spilled down his throat drop by drop until the glass was empty. At that point there was an almighty scream!

A vile dark sprite like creature emerged from Eddies' body its features distorted and ugly. The burning amber eyes bore into mine, with malevolence. The creature like a haze of smoke rose up to the ceiling and disappeared. Eddie put his arms around me, holding me close for the first time, since the episode at Aphrodite's Bath. The warmth of love flooded through me. He pulled away for a second and looked at me as if he hadn't seen me in a long time, then whispered.

'Thank you for saving me Chris.'

We left the pub and walked home. Whatever happened to that evil sprite, I will never find out thankfully. It's my fervent wish that it has been dragged back to the depths of Aphrodite's Bath and will remain there submerged in the darkness forever.

Celia rose from the bench in St Roberts' churchyard. Her brain had so far drawn a blank when it came to new ideas. Some people, well most people actually, thought it more than a little strange that a girl of fifteen years old should spend such a great deal of her free time in the graveyard. There was a comforting air of tranquillity among the gravestones. The peaceful location and normally quiet surroundings, generally enabled her to think of wonderful ideas to turn into short stories. Her mum's voice repeated the words of the past inside her head.

'It's the living you need to be wary of in this life, the dead can do you no harm my love.'

An intense memory of a terrifying nightmare, which had held her in its clutches long after she had awoken caused the hairs to prickle along her scalp. She had been very young at the time and fled horrified from the bed. Alice had woken up long before the child reached her door. Instinct only a mum can possess had filtered through the subconscious alerting her to the little girl's distress. Together mum and daughter returned to Celia's room. A thorough search was made underneath the bed, inside the wardrobe, behind the curtains and every drawer of the chest, ruled out any evidence of hidden monsters. Celia eventually calmed down, allowing Alice to tuck her back into the bed. Sleep stole over her soothing and comforting as a warm blanket. For the remainder of the night her dreams were filled with joyful and wondrous adventures.

Silent tears slipped unbidden down her cheeks caused by the vivid memory of her beloved mum. The ache in her heart was almost too painful to endure. Raw anger mixed with extreme sadness propelled her from the bench. She shouted in defiance towards the Heavens and God for his selfishness. She stood up quickly staring at the sunlight her hands shielding her eyes as she poured out her sorrow.

'Why? Why did you have to take my mum, when I need her so much?'

Though she knew no answer would be forthcoming, the outburst had lessened her anger by some small degree. Deep down inside she understood all too well why her mum had left this world. It was just the end of a life cut short because that was Alice's fate. Destiny determined the length of life, as links in a chain. For the lucky ones the chain was a long one held together with many strong links. Some people managed to live for many years, sometimes reaching far beyond the 3 score years and 10, that's become the average life expectation of a human being. For others the chain is short, the links weak, so much easier to break and the life is ended much sooner than expected.

Since the beginning of time the living have feared death, that dark curtain of nightmares, lurking in our subconscious. There is unawareness of what happens next, or if there is anything more! Those who believed and put faith in the afterlife were fortunate, but many more could not think of a world beyond this one. Faith of any kind is blind, no-one has the ability to see beyond the veil of death. Celia sank to the bench and dabbed the tearstains with a hanky moistened with saliva. It was a good job she didn't wear mascara, panda eyes are not a good look. She thought.

It wasn't as if she had a dad either, he died while she was still a baby. Alice had shown her many photos of John. With his black hair and glittering dark jet like eyes. Celia favoured her father in looks, the resemblance to him was uncanny. Alice told her his death had been even more devastating because he was so young and it was totally unexpected. John at just twenty eight years old had suffered a ruptured appendix and died in the ambulance on the short journey to hospital. Their time together lasted only a brief few years but Alice had told her many times that they were the happiest of her life.

Celia realised it was time to return home, even though Auntie Betty's house never felt like a real home to her. Alice had never mentioned the existence of any relatives, to her daughter. On the day of her mum's funeral Betty had turned up with a bundle of papers proving family connections. She was a distant cousin of Alice, but being in her early 40s, it seemed more appropriate to refer to her as Auntie.

Betty was a highly successful publisher in the city, had never married and had no intention of changing those circumstances anytime soon. She told Celia a family of her own had never been part of her plans for the future. But she did feel it was her duty to offer the girl a place in her home. Blood is thicker than water no matter how diluted the former may be.

It was just a few short weeks since her world had imploded. The pain of grief was raw, like a wound that refused to heal. Auntie Betty provided the basics of food and shelter but that was the full extent of her involvement. She neither offered any affection nor was it sought after. Alice as a mum had so much warmth and was lovingly demonstrative towards her only child. She never lacked an abundance of hugs and a show of affection. She mourned the loss of such great devotion. Once more the tears reigned down, scalding her cheeks and slipping down her neck so that her collar was damp and uncomfortable. Angrily she mopped the tears away with the sodden hanky and walked to the tap in the churchyard. She turned the tap anti-clockwise and the water ran refreshingly cold. Celia splashed her face with the cold clear water until the swelling and redness disappeared from the rims of her eyes.

Smoothing her hair she put her notebook and pen in the bright red and white polka dot leather satchel, which never left her side. It was the last gift received from her mum before she became ill. The happy memory was once again relived of coming home from school on her 15th birthday to find streamers and balloons decorating the kitchen. Her best friends Marcie and Jane along with her mum standing together smiling broadly, their company made the day just perfect. She clutched the bag tightly as if it were about to try and escape. She missed the companionship of Marcie and Jane so much. They wanted to help, but she refused to allow them to get anywhere near. They had loving parents and she had none, envy seethed inside her like a hot poisonous substance, enhancing the lonely existence of her own making. Her heart in contrast had been pierced with a sliver of ice, as far as her so called friends were concerned.

Celia decided she didn't need anyone else in her life now her mum was no longer around. What was the point of loving people, they only went and died on you? With a heavy heart she forced herself to visit her parents' grave.

'Sorry I didn't mean that mum and dad, it wasn't your fault. You couldn't help dying. I just miss you both so much!'

As she spoke the words a gentle breeze stirred the petals in the rose vase of the headstone. An ice cold shiver sped swiftly along her spine as if chasing some imaginary foe. She was suddenly aware of a tingle of warmth attempting to thaw the ice barrier, which had formed a protective shield around her heart. A whisper so quiet as to be almost imaginary floated towards her, almost like a gentle kiss on the cheek. She stood still, listening intently sure she was imagining the barely audible voice. The whisper gathered strength as the volume slowly but painstakingly became louder. It was becoming more audible by the second until the words were properly understood. The voice belonged to Alice and her words were now unmistakably clear!

'Celia, open the door....'

The voice came to an abrupt stop as if the connection had been broken. She reeled in shock and almost stumbled in her sheer haste to flee the graveyard.

She ran as if pursued by demons until her legs almost buckled underneath her and breathing became painful as she gasped. A painful stitch in her side caused her to suddenly stop. Then slowly the realisation of what she had heard shocked her to the core. There was no mistake, it was not a figment of her imagination! Celia had distinctly heard the voice of her mum from beyond the grave. But for the time being the words spoken made no sense. Her heart beat so fast it was like the fluttering wings of a humming bird inside her chest.

Oh why did I run away maybe she would have spoken again? Why is it when I have longed to hear her voice, did the sound of it strike me with sheer terror? Well the answer to that was simple enough; no-one least of all me; expected any sort of communication with the dead. It was time to get back to the house. Auntie Betty would be wondering where she had got to. A glance at her watch showed that she had been away for four hours. The hours had slipped by faster than grains of sand slipping through a timer. Not one word had she written down in her notebook in all that time, her thought processes blocked. But that had changed dramatically she had more than enough to think about right now. Her imagination was running on overdrive.

Betty paced the floor of her pristine white kitchen, she really was very annoyed with her niece. She had spent ages cooking a wonderful roast dinner and it was now ruined. Celia had been told to be back at 2pm sharp it was now 4 15pm. Betty stopped pacing and took a sip from her coffee cup. Calm down Betty it is only a meal that has been spoiled. You don't want to make too much fuss when the girl gets back, that's if she does come back? The sudden thought provided her with cause for concern. Before she could pursue the thought any further the front door opened then slammed shut. Celia hurried into the kitchen her cheeks flushed, her breathing laboured as if she had been running too fast. She gulped a few times and held her side as if in pain.

'I'm so sorry Auntie the time just slipped away. I really didn't mean to be late!'

'Never mind Celia the only thing ruined is the dinner. I can order a take-away for us what would you like?'

'I love Chinese food me and mum used to go to Chinese Restaurants on special occasions...'

Betty thought the girl was about to say more but the memories conjured up, caused a sad expression to form on the girl's lovely face and halted the words she was about to speak.

'Chinese it is then. Would you mind helping me clear up the kitchen first Celia?'

Later that same evening after the meal had been consumed in silence, Betty had asked Celia how she'd spent the afternoon. Celia lied to her Auntie, telling her she had spent the last few hours with friends. She helped clear away the dishes and then headed straight to her room.

The house was modern and looked clinical to Celia's eyes, no homely touches or warm colours to brighten the place up. It was decorated entirely in shades of black and white from the carpets to the furniture, the walls and even the curtains. Her room was the only place in the house which held any hint of colour. The curtains were a sunny shade of yellow to match the bedding. Apart from that small concession everything else in the room was in varying shades of white. Celia sat on the bed and pondered the episode in the graveyard. Had it really been her mother's voice or just imagination playing a cruel trick at her expense? She decided to write the details in her notebook and then tackle her homework it was Sunday and time was not on her side. A knock at the door made her jump.

'Celia I have to go out for a while. I have a meeting with my latest novelist, back in a couple of hours, three, at the most. Will you be alright?'

'Yes I'll be fine thanks, I have my homework to finish. Goodbye Auntie.'

The homework assignments were quickly finished and her things for school the following day all prepared and laid out for the morning. Her auntie had still not returned and Celia decided now was the time to have a proper look around the house. Since she arrived at the house her interest in the new surroundings had been non- existent, yet now she suddenly had a burning curiosity to explore and try to find out something about Betty. The imaginative side of her had conjured up so many ideas concerning her Auntie. She could have just asked questions but stubbornly refused to try and be anything, other than the stroppy uncooperative lonely, grieving teenager, with a massive chip on her shoulders. Angry with the whole world.

She left her bedroom and peaked inside the two guest rooms. The beds were neatly made ready for any would be guest but the wardrobes and chests of drawers were completely empty. In the main bathroom the medicine cabinet contained little apart from toothpaste and toiletries. She was curious to know about the contents inside Betty's own bedroom but would not dream of invading her privacy. Just as she was sure her Auntie respected her own need for privacy.

Downstairs in the living room there was a large white glossy sideboard, but the contents of the drawers were sparse and there was nothing she could bring herself to investigate. There were a few photos to look at, but in the main the drawers contained notebooks, pens and letters, she was not the kind of person to read someone's private mail.   The kitchen cupboards turned up nothing of interest either. She was about to give up and go to her room when she spotted the strange door next to the utility room, how odd, she thought! She was certain that there had been no door there before, and this one was out of place with the rest of the room. The door looked ancient it was of dark wood with iron hinges and a looped handle. A heavy lock underneath the handle held an ornate key shiny from constant use. She was drawn forward by intense curiosity but also hesitant, unexpectedly afraid. Where had the door appeared from? It definitely hadn't been there earlier when she had helped her Auntie clear away the dinner dishes. She was certain of that fact, she also knew that it did not belong in this pristine, glossy white, designer kitchen. A sound from the hallway sent her scurrying out of the kitchen. The key turned in the lock and she almost felt faint until the door opened and Betty stepped into the hall.

'Celia sorry to be so late you should be in bed by now though. Off you go goodnight.'

Betty briefly put her arm around the girl's shoulder but Celia shrugged it away immediately and felt ashamed when she saw the hurt look in her Auntie's eyes. She ran up the stairs her face burning red, but still determined to keep the ice barrier in place around her heart. She was going to write down her thoughts in the notebook but fell asleep almost instantly. The dream wove its way into her subconscious and she heard a voice calling out to her from a great distance.

'Please help Celia!'

She opened her eyes and was standing in a low ceilinged windowless corridor. The walls were lined in panels of dark wood, the floor was covered in black and white tiles. There was a thick layer of dust on the floor tiles and cobwebs hung from the ceiling. She turned around but was unable to see anything behind her through darkness so dense it was frightening. From ahead a light gradually grew brighter and she could see the outline of a door. She ran quickly in her haste to escape who or what lurked in the darkness of the dusty corridor. When she reached the door she stopped in her tracks, it was the same door she had seen in the kitchen that mysteriously appeared and then promptly vanished. She could not face the fear of opening that door, even though the voice called out to her with a pitiful urgency.

'Please help Celia I need you!'

Every night for the past week the same dream had been played out in her sleeping hours but never progressed. Celia was too fearful of what she might find beyond the ancient wooden door. It was Sunday again and she grabbed her satchel and left the house promising her Auntie Betty faithfully, to be back in time for tea. The week had been a difficult one and not just because of the dreams. The loneliness weighed heavy on her shoulders dragging down her spirit to even greater depths. Auntie Betty was noticeably changing since Celia had moved in to share her home. Each day she tried that little bit harder to get to know Celia and offer the hand of friendship to the lost teenager. Celia could not allow herself to get too close and made sure the ice barrier encasing her heart would not have cause to thaw out.

She had brought flowers to place in the vase on her parent's grave. They were golden yellow roses, the petals like miniature bursts of sunshine the sight of them even caused Celia to smile. She took the dead flowers from the rose vase and put them on the compost pile in the corner of the churchyard, then filled the vase with fresh water from the tap. As she made her way back she thought someone called out to her. The voice was familiar she had heard it in her dreams. It was her mum! She started to run back towards her parent's grave, the voice seemed to be following her but there was no-one there. At the grave she shivered as the voice called out to her in a pleading tone.

'Celia help me please, you have to open the door!'

The words as before stopped abruptly communication came to an abrupt end. A soft breeze stirred the petals of the roses turning the golden yellow to an even deeper brighter shade. Fear was quickly replaced by wonder. Celia could feel her mum's arms in a brief loving embrace, the warmth of it seeped into her heart. She arranged the flowers and made a silent promise. Later at home Betty was amazed when Celia walked into the kitchen and said.

'Hello Auntie Betty, have you had a good afternoon?'

The few words were accompanied by a very fleeting but so very heart -
warming smile. Celia went to bed early that night and quickly drifted into the
now familiar occurring dream. The corridor appeared exactly the same as before
and the darkness behind her no less dense, but somehow the fear had
evaporated, she was ready to face the next step. The door appeared ahead the
outline of which glowed brightly the voice beyond it had gathered in strength.

'Celia will you please open the door now?'

She stretched out a hand and turned the key in the lock half expecting the
handle to give out electric shocks or something even worse. The door creaked
slightly causing her to flinch. As she stepped through the doorway, a wonderful
bright light bathed her in a warm glow, courage surged through her body,
dissipating any trace of her earlier fears. The scene before her was amazingly
magnificent she stepped into a wood with trees of purple, blue and pink,
growing tall and strong. The leaves glittered like diamonds the carpet of moss
on the ground was the colour of gold dust. Celia walked along the path through
the trees until she came to a clearing. There stood a circle of life sized canvases
with an opening gap between just large enough for Celia to fit through. Sun
streamed down through the trees bathing the whole scene in light of such
brilliance she had never seen before.

She ran towards the circle and slipped through the gap. Her eyes sparkled
in sheer admiration at the amazing sights before her. She gazed at the first
canvas, it was a painting of the back view of a young woman with long red hair
wearing a dress of white silk. In turn Celia walked to each canvas and the young
woman was turning ever so slightly as if twirling gently in a form of dance. At
last the beautiful features were visible and Celia was amazed to see the face of
her mum as she appeared in the photographs of her wedding day. The beautiful
tiara of pearls made her appearance like that of a princess. Tears trickled down
Celia's face at the sight of her mum. A smile spread across Alice's face and she

stepped from the canvas and gathered her daughter in her arms. The pair hugged each other tightly in a close embrace and then Alice spoke.

'Celia my love, so glad you are here. I called you because I need your help to find your dad John. I have been kept prisoner in the canvases up until now. But your courage and strength has set me free. Can I rely on you to help me find John?'

'Of course mum I would do anything to help you and dad. I love you so much.'

The pair set off right away through the forest. The further they walked the more dark and dense it became. Celia was unafraid, just knowing her mum needed her help gave her the courage to face any danger. She suddenly wondered where she had found the power to set her mum free, but dismissed the thought quickly after all this was a dream. Anything is possible in a dream. A large tree crashed down a little way ahead of them, the shock waves reverberating throughout the forest. Birds rose up and flew away rapidly as if in fear. The tree was so dense they struggled to climb over it.

The forest was very dark, but it was possible to see the colours of the trees were no longer of bright vibrant colours. The sound of horses galloping through the forest drove Celia and her mum into finding a hiding place behind a large bush. As the riders drew near they could be seen clearly as chinks of light suddenly and unexpectedly pierced the darkness. Alice and Celia both quietly gasped in shock when they spotted John sat on a horse, his hands were tied and a rope was draped around his neck. The other two riders were wearing dark helmets and black cloaks making it impossible to see their features. The horses came to a stop the riders dismounted, then roughly pulled John from his to be thrown to the ground. They quickly tied him securely to a tree and set about making a fire, they were settling in for the night.

'You won't escape this time John we will camp here tonight. Enjoy the rest, there is a long way to travel tomorrow.'

Hours passed slowly, the camp fire died down eventually and the captors had finally fallen asleep. Celia and Alice stretched their limbs which ached from the inactivity of the past few hours. Alice had found it unbearable watching John being badly treated and not being able to offer him any help. But Celia had told her to be patient, it was too dangerous to make a move so soon they might all be killed. The men who held John prisoner were armed with swords. Celia and Alice had no weapons to defend themselves. Alice and Celia carefully and deliberately grabbed the swords and pulled them free of the scabbards of the sleeping captors. Alice went to John and shook him awake, her fingers to her lips to signal for him to keep silent. John thought he must be dreaming until she cut the ropes from his neck and wrists. He hugged her for a brief moment and they moved towards the sleeping captors, unaware that their prisoner was just about to make his escape once more as they slept, swiftly John and Alice securely tied their wrists with the very rope that had earlier bound his own so tightly.   The skin was broken and the wounds around his wrists wet with fresh blood. Alice ripped a couple of strips from the hem of her dress and bound his wounds, not just from compassion for her husband, but not wanting to leave a trail of blood spots to lead the enemy their way. They were lucky to have the horses to make their escape.

Alice, Celia and John mounted the horses and soon left the camp and the captors far behind. They rode off as fast as the forest path would allow. Soon they were headed towards the very outer edge of the forest. The circle of canvases was their place of safety. The further they rode back towards that clearing the lighter the forest became. The trees of vibrant bright colours was closer now. The fallen tree was soon reached, the horses easily jumped over the fallen mass. Once more they all caught sight of the circle of canvases in the clearing ahead. The brilliant light illuminating the scene in all its magnificence. They arrived safely at the circle. Just in time it seemed, as the sound of many horses hooves galloping through the dark forest was heard. Alice and John hugged their daughter in turn and though the encounter was brief, she knew the memory would have to last a lifetime and didn't doubt that it would sustain her in the future.

'Celia you have set us free, now it is time to leave. We will meet again one day. You have a great deal of life left to live so don't waste it in grief. Open the door and you will find happiness.'

Alice and John stepped into the main canvas together and suddenly all the paintings changed. In each one was a picture of Alice and John enjoying the lives they had loved and lived together. The first painting showed them on the day they met. The next canvas was a painting of the couple on the day of their engagement. In the third painting they were stood outside the church of St Roberts, smiling for the photographer. Alice dressed in white silk, the sun glinting off the pearl tiara causing her hair to shine as though stardust had been scattered through the glossy strands, John looked so smart in his grey suit with a yellow rose in his button hole to match those in the bridal bouquet.

Alice quickly took in the details of each canvas and became aware of the ice melting the barrier around her heart setting it free to find love again. It was now time to make the best of a life which was far too precious to waste. There was so much to look forward to, life was filled with adventures, you just had to have the courage to go out and make things happen. There was a great future ahead of her if she was prepared to go out and find it. Auntie Betty and her friends had tried to help and she had treated them all so coldly. The poisonous envy had now evaporated, her heart no longer encased in ice was ready to let the warmth of affection in, she felt young and free as only a fifteen year old should.

She would apologise to them all for her mean and selfish behaviour and hope that they would be willing to accept it.

The galloping horses were drawing so near she feared being caught. As she gazed at the last canvas in the circle, her parents' waived goodbye then vanished from sight. She turned around to find the ancient door behind her and she grabbed the handle turning it quickly and stepping through to the safety of the corridor. She took one last look at the scene beyond. The circle of canvases had begun to shimmer and fade. The trees vanished one by one, a bright light appeared so blinding it blocked out all trace of the wood which had been so vivid in colour. The beam of light exploded, slamming the door shut with a deafeningly loud crash. The shining key turned slowly: locking the door, before it completely disappeared. The dream ended but the memories would last throughout the whole of Celia's life!

'Timothy!'

Lily called out for him with a high-pitched shrill sound. You would think it was a matter of life and death that he come to her right now, this very second. Judging by that tone of voice. He was just a couple of metres away from the campervan. He was actually visibly cringing with embarrassment, noticing the other campers had turned their gaze towards the sound of that voice, which could shatter fine crystal.

What kind of a name was Timothy for goodness sake? He was a teenager. Teenagers weren't supposed to be called Timothy, not the sort who were popular anyway! Lily could have shortened it to Tim. Okay Tim was not much of a name either, it was alright for some but did not suit him one bit. Still Tim was a slight improvement and sounded nowhere near as wimpy in his estimation as Timothy. Once more the squeaky voice rang out with surprising strength and he squirmed, wishing it were possible to just disappear.

'Timothy my darling, where are you?'

Oh no! Not darling; this was just too much. The flushing heat of embarrassment quickly spread throughout his body, finally causing his ears to twitch with agitation. If she had bothered to glance through the window of the campervan it would have been no problem to catch sight of him. But something that simply practical would never have occurred to her. Okay, okay, he thought. Suddenly feeling a twinge of guilt for causing her concern. I understand she is elderly, and a grandmother and she deserves to be respected. I am very fond of her, he thought. Yet it still didn't alter the fact that he was now seventeen years old. A seventeen year old who just happened to have the worst kind luck being named Timothy. A seventeen year old, who had the disadvantage of spending, a long Bank Holiday weekend in a campervan at Brecon with a couple of grandparents.

I am old enough to take care of myself, old enough to be trusted. Why couldn't I have been allowed to stay at home? It's just not fair!

It seemed to Tim, yes Tim! Not Timothy; that not much in life was fair when you were seventeen. He had looked forward to growing older and becoming a teenager but it wasn't how he expected it to be. He wanted adventure but life was just ordinary most of the time. His thoughts turned to Rosie as they certainly always did, on a very frequent basis. If he had been allowed to remain at home, he and Rosie could have made good use of their time together all alone. This train of thought gave him a glimmer of happiness, yet is was to be cut short as once more he heard his name being called in a voice with a heightened sense of urgency.

'Timothy where are you? If you don't come here right now there will be no dinner for you, I mean it!'

The accustomed frequent pangs of hunger gnawed at is empty stomach and he slunk back to the campervan for dinner. Another thing, he thought when the food was eaten and his stomach comfortingly full again. No offence intended, but three bodies inside a tiny campervan did not make for a decently congenial environment. The bodily odours were closely mingled and not in the least bit pleasant, especially to someone like himself with such an acute sense of smell.

Once again he slunk back outside and breathed in deeply of the fresh clean air of the Brecon Beacons. It certainly was a wonderful place to be, if that is; you were allowed the freedom to explore the surroundings. He sat still for a long while just letting his thoughts run away, his mind thinking of anything and nothing very much in particular. He noticed a middle aged woman walking along the path towards the main site ablutions block. She gazed into his eyes as if seeing straight into his heart and soul, instantly sensing the emotions he felt.

She smiled warmly and somehow knowingly, as if all too aware of his plight and conveyed empathy in her calm blue eyes. It was a fleeting moment of recognition, but made quite a big impression on him. He returned her gaze for just a second then looked away.

His thoughts were filled with the image of the woman. His imagination running away with him. I am almost certain that she would never make a teenager spend a whole weekend, and a long one at that, in a campervan with grandparents. I feel sure she would have felt more compassion for a youngster who happened to be in love and didn't want to be parted from his lovely girlfriend Rosie.

Still the sun was shining and he was outside in the fresh air. He would just put the grandparents out of mind and explore the surroundings. There were plenty of places of interest close by. In that instant another campervan arrived on the site and stopped just in front of him. It reversed into the vacant space next door to the one Lily and her husband occupied.

The door opened and a youngish couple stepped from the cab, followed by a teenager. He couldn't help but catch sight of the beautiful golden Labrador. All thoughts of Rosie were instantly banished from his mind and he stared in wonder and admiration at the good looking female dog. She caught his stare and instantly sensed his admiration and obvious interest in getting to know her. Things were starting to become much more interesting, Tim thought. Maybe this weekend was not going to be so bad after all. Things were definitely looking so much brighter.

A weekend stuck with the oldies in a campervan was never going to appeal to any teenager, especially a young dog named Tim with romance and a sense of adventure in mind. But the warm gaze he was receiving from that lovely Labrador was a sure sign that they were both about to embark on a wonderful adventure indeed. He stood up proudly displaying his shiny dark coat. With a fresh sense of purpose Tim made his way towards the next door neighbour with the golden hair.

Emma

The scream, razor sharp; sliced through the misty grey curtain of sleep. Helen
was shaken into awareness, already she was on the alert to impending danger.
Jim mercifully, slept on undisturbed. He would have to wake up soon enough.
There was a busy twelve hour shift, ahead of him at the manufacturing plant. It
was important that he get plenty of rest before the busy day began.

Helen glanced briefly at the luminous clock face and confirmed it was
precisely 3 o'clock. These past fourteen nights since the 8th of May, had
gradually developed into a living nightmare. The dreadful sounds of ear-
splitting screams; proclaimed the all too familiar alarm call from their five year
old daughter Emma. At precisely the same time; every single night without fail.
This horrible reoccurring incident during the darkest hours, before the merciful
light of dawn, added to the fear and terror if it were at all possible to feel any
worse.

Within seconds of waking she reached the little girls' bedside. The child's
face was distorted into a mask of pure terror. Her facial features barely
recognisable; small fists tightly clenched, knuckles bleached white, she fought
off the invisible attacker. Anguished screams of terror poured forth from the
little girl.

Helen scooped the child into her arms rocking the small body gently back
and forth, murmuring words of comfort, smoothing the furrows from the little
girls' fevered brow. The screams eventually diminished. The child limp as a rag
doll sagged against her mothers' body, features once more relaxed. Her
eyelashes fluttered rapidly as dark butterfly wings. Then became still to rest
above tear stained cheeks, at last peace resumed.

With an aching heaviness; silent sobs shuddered through her body threatening hysteria. The child's suffering a dagger repeatedly stabbing her heart. Despair and frustration battled heartache and pure grief. She was both mother and sentinel. It was her job to fight all the baddies; slay the dragons; turn dark to light; tears to laughter; kiss and hug pain until it shrivelled and died. But most important of all, it was her prime task to love this child more than life itself. For the remainder of the night she held Emma safe in her arms, defying the unseen night terrors to return.

A light tap on the shoulder awoke her for the second time. Jim carefully removed the sleeping child from her arms. He tucked his daughter into bed and kissed the dark brown silky curls on top of her head.

'It's half past five. I have to go now. There's a cup of tea on the bedside table. Try and get some rest you look worn out, see you this evening, bye love.'

His arms briefly wrapped her in a warm, reassuring, blanket of comfort. The fleeting hug was so very welcome, after the long dark night spent in cold despair. It was after he left, that she realised he'd received no word of thanks for the tea, let alone a 'goodbye'.

A couple of hours sleep would be welcome but that wasn't possible now. She was wound up as tightly as a coiled spring. Bees swarmed noisily in every chamber of her brain. They swarmed noisily spreading out, crowding every centimetre of space. There was no peace to be found, the sweet oblivion of sleep was not an option.

She busied herself in preparation for the day ahead. This situation with Emma could not be allowed to continue. Help was needed, professional help. Sometime today, Helen was determined to book an appointment, with Dr Williams at the hospital. She would explain in detail everything, which had been happening to Emma. He must be able to find a solution to the problem. Steely determination strengthened her resolve. Warrior like she was prepared to fight tooth and nail, to undertake whatever task was required in order to help her precious little daughter.

As if on cue Emma came bounding into the room; and launched herself into her mothers' arms. She drenched Helen's cheeks with sloppy wet kisses; python like chubby arms crept around her neck. The little girls' eyes shone like rays of bright sunlight. It was almost as if the night terrors had never transpired. Each and every morning, Helen asked her daughter the same question.

'Did you have a bad dream last night sweetheart?' Every day the answer remained the same.

'No mummy, no bad dream.'

Emma sat at the kitchen table. Between eating mouthfuls of cereal she chattered excitedly to the doll perched on a chair next to hers. There was no resemblance between this bright little bundle of joy and the haunted, tortured soul of twilight hours.

One month later, Helen, Jim and Emma sat patiently in the waiting room at the hospital. All of their hopes were pinned on this appointment with the Psychologist. Minutes later a nurse popped her head around the door.

'Mr Garside will see you now.'

The room was filled with light, and comfortable furniture, it was more like a cosy lounge than a surgery. Mr Garside's greeting was full of warmth and reassurance. He took the parents to one side while the nurse kept the little girls attention occupied with a picture book.

'I can understand and sympathise with the concern you have, regarding your daughter. Mr Williams gave me a brief outline regarding the problem. Let me assure you both, hypnotherapy is a safe option. Statistically it's proven to have been very successful in helping children. For very young children hypnotherapy is much less traumatic than asking direct questions. Whatever lurks in the subconscious will be the key needed to unlock the cause of her night terrors.'

Emma snuggled comfortably on to her mothers' lap. Mr Garside spoke softly for just a few seconds while concentrating his gaze directly into the child's eyes. Almost immediately her eyelashes began to flutter, the lids closed and the child relaxed visibly.

'Emma can you hear me? I want to ask you some questions.'

Helen and Jim shuddered in unison. Ice cold fingers crawled slowly but surely tracing a path the length of their spines. The child in her mothers' arms spoke in a voice which was totally unrecognisable to either parent. They looked at each other with a mixture of genuine fear and astonishment as the unfamiliar voice spoke up.

The voice that of a young child sounded agitated and very much afraid. Helen felt both empathy and sadness listening to the words.

'Who is Emma? My name is Jessica!'

Mr Garside glanced at Helen and Jim their features frozen mirrors reflecting the same expression. He turned off the tape recorder.

'I'm guessing neither of you are familiar with this voice. With your permission I'll carry on with the questions. The child is more receptive than I could have hoped for!'

'Please feel free to carry on. There has to be an end to the terror our daughter is suffering every single night. We will try anything, as long as it helps.'

The Doctor switched on the recorder and resumed the questions.

'Can you tell me where you are Emma?'

'I don't know anyone called Emma! My name is Jessica. I don't know where I am. It's so cold and it's very dark. I'm scared because I can't see anything.'

'How did you get there Emma, do you know?'

'No I don't know and I'm not Emma.'

The voice was silent for a few seconds then spoke up, in an excited, angry voice.

'It must be her fault. She stopped my breath. She put her hands over my mouth and stopped my breath. I tried to fight back but she was too big and strong. I want my mummy and daddy it's horrible here!'

Suddenly Emma wept silent tears the small body was rigid in the arms of her mother. Helens' stomach suddenly turned ice cold. She hugged the child tight as if she were a lifebelt, trying to put an end to the drowning sensation within. Mr Garside asked another question.

'Jessica who was it that hurt you?'

'The nurse hurt me. She told mummy and daddy not to worry. Told them I would get better soon. When they left, she stopped my breath. I don't know how to find them.'

'Jessica what's your last name?'

'Jessica Soames.'

'Do you remember the name of the hospital you were in?'

'The Royal Infa-mary.'

'Do you mean the Royal Infirmary?'

'Yes! That's what I said, The Infa-mary. Can I see mummy and daddy now?'

That pitifully pleading, sad childish voice, touched the hearts of all those assembled in the consulting room.

'You can rest now Jessica go back to sleep.'

Emma's tears stopped flowing abruptly. The dark lashes fluttered gently as she opened her eyes. A loud yawn escaped through the soft lips. Her limbs stretched out as if they had been immobile for a very long time.

'Mummy please can I have a biscuit. My belly is growling again?' Jim rushed over to his wife and daughter enfolding them in a warm embrace.

'You can have as many biscuits as you like sweetheart.'

Five weeks had sped by since the hypnotherapy session with Mr Garside. Emma had ceased to suffer from the terrorising and frequent nightmares that same day. Peace reigned over the household by day and every night was tranquil without incident. The little girl slept right through each night, waking up every single morning refreshed and cheerful. She was bright eyed and happy just as a small child should be. Emma had not a care in the world. Helen and Jim felt the pure relief of a great weight having been lifted from both their hearts and minds.

It was the day of Emma's hospital appointment with Dr Williams, for a routine examination. After a long delay due to over running appointments Helen was grateful, when the nurse stepped from his consulting room and called out the child's name.

Dr Williams gestured for mother and daughter to take a seat. He then asked the nurse to distract Emma's attention for a few moments. He took the mother aside and spoke to Helen keeping his voice low.

'I must admit it was a terrible shock to read the newspaper article, concerning the arrest of the nurse, from the children's ward at the Royal Infirmary. It's inconceivable to myself how a member of the medical profession could do such a terrible thing. Thank God the police caught her before she could commit another murder. Strange though how the knowledge of her crimes came to light. There was no mention of any witnesses!'

He shook his head in disbelief that anyone could murder a defenceless child. He suspected that somehow Emma had been involved in naming the murderess, given his knowledge of the victim but kept his thoughts to himself. Helen's thinking mirrored his own in fact. But she decided not to mention the details of the hypnotherapy session, or Emma's involvement in the investigation. Although it hadn't been Emma who told the story of a murder having been committed! A cold shiver ran down her spine at the memory of that unknown child's voice. It had been heart wrenching to hear the despair in one so young.

'Now Emma, let me take a look at that scar.'

The long livid scar in the middle of the child's chest was fading a little more each time he checked it.

'It's certainly healing very well and the medication is working out fine. There is no reason why this new heart should not last a lifetime. Please make an appointment at reception for one month from today.'

Helen helped Emma to get dressed and thanked Mr Williams as always, before they left his consulting room.

She had spent the past five weeks carrying out extensive research, both at the library and via the internet. There were a good many incidents of (Cellular Memory). It was a strange phenomenon that some transplant recipients retained certain aspects of their donor's memories. The stories were too numerous to be without real substance. The more she read the more she was convinced of the truth of these somewhat fantastic accounts. Each story was investigated thoroughly and there was no evidence to suggest that the details could be fabricated.

When the police had arrested the nurse she vehemently denied murdering Jessica but they were convinced of her guilt. A thorough investigation, soon uncovered the truth and she was now in prison awaiting trial. It was highly likely she would be not only be found guilty, but also receive a long sentence, befitting the seriousness of her crime.

The child's spirit could now rest in peace. Her parents had been through hell since the nurse was arrested. They found it was almost impossible to deal with the feelings of guilt, over the tragic fate of their young daughter. Yet in their hearts they knew that the horrific outcome was beyond their control. They could not have dreamed their precious child would be murdered in the very hospital ward where she was sent to be nursed back to health.

Helen became more and more convinced by the existence of (Cellular Memory). Since the hypnotherapy session Emma's' personality had changed both subtly but very evidently. She was still a loving happy child, but she often spoke of things which were a complete mystery to her parents. She would speak of days out, and reminisce about holidays in locations that the family had never visited. These memories must have belonged to Jessica. It was more than a little unnerving to hear the recollections that were not her own.

Helen asked if she could be told the identity of their child's organ donor. Though details of the murder trial was published in the newspapers, they had not been permitted to mention the victim's personal details not even her name. After insisting that she needed to know the name of the donor who had given her daughter a heart: the parents were contacted. It was a great relief when they gave their permission to get in contact.

It was not that much of a surprise to learn Emma had been the recipient of Jessica's heart. Helen and Jim decided the least they could do was thank them personally, for the precious gift of life their child had received from Jessica. The Soames were so grateful for their visit. Among other things, Helen learned that Jessica's date of birth was May the 8th. The very same date that Emma's nightmares had begun. Helen was convinced that somehow this date was the trigger for the dead child's memories to manifest in their own daughter.

May the 8th one year later. The four adults seated on the patio in wicker chairs revelled in the warm sunshine. All four pairs of eyes turned towards the child playing happily in the garden. Her dark brown curls bouncing as she ran around, small face flushed with the effort and shining with joy. The two couples had formed a great friendship, which had begun that first time Helen and Jim had visited the Soames' house. Mrs Soames unconsciously patted her swollen stomach, a look of contentment on her face pretty face. She could hardly wait to hold a new baby in her arms. As if on cue she felt the kicking of her baby reassuringly strong. It was due any day now. This baby represented so much hope for the future. He or she would expel the remainder of the black despair which clung fiercely to the parents aching hearts. Though she and Jessica's father would forever mourn the loss of their little girl. It was comforting to know that a part of her lived on in Emma.

Emma stopped running. She stood perfectly still for a few seconds as if frozen to the spot. She appeared to be listening intently to an unseen presence. After a couple of minutes she laughed loudly before bursting into song. She sang out loud while twirling in a circle hands held out as if holding on to someone or something.

'Happy Birthday to you. Happy Birthday to you. Happy Birthday dear Jessica!

Happy Birthday to you!'

Helen and Jim looked towards their daughter. Their expressions of shock mirroring each other as they recognised the voice of the singer. Memories of the hypnotherapy session came flooding back and with it the voice of the dead child. The same voice that now sung the birthday song. Not their daughter Emma but that of the deceased Jessica Soames.

70th Anniversary of D Day   6th of June 2014.

Vera had spent more than an hour getting ready before leaving the house. She had always taken great pride in her appearance. Today was no exception, but it was obviously even more important for her to look the best she could on this very special day.

Her memories drifted slowly in reverse down the long winding lane of time. She smiled at the recollection of that wonderful day almost a lifetime ago, that she remembered so vividly, as if it were yesterday. The day she would dearly love to relive, that wonderful day when Teddy had declared the depth of his love and devotion for her. That love still endured all these years later and the bright spark of it still glowed deep within her heart.

28th of May 1944

Teddy and Vera had spent the warm, sunny, completely idyllic day together. Time more precious now than it had ever been, was running past far too quickly. Everyone had to live for the day during war time, never knowing if there would even be a tomorrow. Teddy had just a few treasured days left of his leave. He was a soldier in the tank regiment based at Brockenhurst, in the New Forest.

They had been for a picnic in the woods close to home. Though rations were in short supply, Vera's mother had been saving the coupons to ensure the couple had a few little treats. They later walked home through the woods arms linked together. They each remained silent knowing that time would not slow down its pace. The dreaded parting would come along all too soon. Abruptly Teddy came to a standstill. The sun shone down throughout a clearing between the trees, bathing them in a golden haze of light.

He pulled Vera into his arms and kissed her with a fierce passion willing the moment to last an eternity. Vera loved him with an intensity which was sometimes frightening, she felt her very life depended on him being near. Each time they parted it was as if she died a little and only regained her full life force on his return. He pulled away suddenly and dropped to the ground on one knee. He gazed deep into her eyes almost searching her heart to see if the love she had for him was as strong and bright as his own. He dipped a hand into his jacket pocket and pulled out a little box. She gasped at the sheer surprise, her answer already decided before he even asked.

'Vera marry me I love you so much, we can get a special license. There is no more time left to waste. I am going over to France to join the 8th Armoured Brigade next Monday!'

'Of course I will marry you Teddy. I love you with all my heart!'

He slid the solitaire diamond ring on to her slender finger and they hugged and kissed with all the enthusiasm and sheer joy that only love can bring.

At the end of the evening their dreams were shattered into a million pieces. George, Vera's father would not give his 17 year old daughter consent to marry. No matter how decent a young man Teddy was she was much too young. There was the matter of the world war to consider. A veteran of the Great War he was no stranger to the horrors of combat. He had seen the death of many members of his regiment. He had also seen many maimed their wounds sickening. So many soldiers with no visible wounds were surely mentally scarred for the remainder of their lives, by the terrible scenes witnessed. He shuddered at his own vivid memories of the horrors seen in battle.

'Teddy I know you are a decent chap and believe you love my daughter, but if you marry and God forbid don't survive the war, what happens to her?

Please see this situation from my point of view. I'm only thinking of my girl. When the war is over I promise to give you both the most wonderful wedding possible and you will have both mine and Sadie's blessing!'

Vera sobbed in Teddy's arms. She felt her heart would break, the pain was unbearable. The young man felt the powerlessness of youth against authority. There was nothing they could do but wait until the war ended and who knew when that would be. Vera's mother Sadie looked at the young couple clinging on to each other, her eyes filled with tears at the sadness and dejection she saw mirrored in their faces. But she had to agree with George's decision.

They had wanted to marry before he left for the trenches of France in the Great War, but neither her own nor Georges' parents would give them their consent. Sadie thought they were just too old, too selfish, or had forgotten what it felt like to be in love. She had been heartbroken at the time but now felt ashamed of the behaviour meted out towards her own parents back then. Now she understood all too clearly the reason for their reluctance in consenting to the marriage. Though it hurt no less to see her daughter's suffering, she understood all too well every bit of the pain Vera was feeling. Teddy shook Georges' hand.

'I love Vera so much. I can see you won't relent and give us your blessing. We have no choice but to wait. I am going over to France next week to join the 8th Armoured Brigade. Please carry on taking good care of my girl. I will be back soon enough so you better start saving for that wedding!'

The older man shook his hand warmly and briefly placed a hand on the young mans' shoulder.

'Good luck Teddy, we will pray for your safe return every single day.'

He left the young couple alone in the living room as he and Sadie went upstairs. Even when they reached their bedroom at the back of the house it was impossible to ignore the   great heart wrenching sobs of their daughter and both felt deep pity for her and Teddy. Sadie wept knowing the pain that young couple were suffering and George held her close until the tears stopped falling.

2014

Vera felt the burning sensation of tears threatening to escape, and flow freely down her cheeks. The memory of that long ago day with Teddy both delightful and yet so bittersweet.

She was now 87 years old, it had been a long life. Often she had speculated on how things would have turned out; if only they had been permitted to marry before Teddy left for France. She mentally reprimanded herself, for being a sentimental and fanciful old woman. 'It was pointless to dwell on what might have been Vera.'

She whispered to herself, now dressed in her best clothes, she checked her reflection in the mirror. Not bad for an old lady, she thought. After all these years she was still tall, slim, and straight backed. She smiled hearing once again her mother's voice, from the distant past repeatedly saying to her.

'Vera. Stand up straight, shoulders back, head up, be proud of your height don't try to hide it!'

Every single day of her life she had done just that, stood up straight and proud even when she had felt pain so deep, she thought it would crush her spirit. So many of the people she had known and loved were now long gone. She had been alone for many years, but now understood all too well, what it truly felt like to be completely and utterly abandoned. There were no family members left, her one and only friend had died just a couple of weeks previously.

She picked up the photo in the silver gilt frame that had stood for so many years on her dressing table. The face she gazed at every waking morning and kissed fondly every night before retiring to sleep. Teddy in his uniform at just 19 years old, the fresh face of a young man untouched by blemishes. His forehead smooth and free of worry lines under the slicked back, brill-creamed quiff of blonde hair. The eyes alight with the enthusiasm of youth and the promise of a long and eventful life ahead. Though the photo was monochrome her memory filled the likeness with colour, the smattering of a few brown freckles along his nose and cheek. The slightly tanned skin complimented by the brightest most beautiful blue eyes she had ever seen. She planted a kiss on the frame were his lips smiled that day in a brief moment in time, a snapshot of a scene, one of many that make up a lifetime. It was then she gazed at the laughing girl by his side, her arms linked in his, gazing up at the exceptionally tall youth with adoration. The flower patterned cotton summer dress fluttered slightly at the hem showing off tanned legs and white sandals. The girl had her hair styled in the victory roll, but the breeze had caused some of the pins to loosen and little tendrils had escaped framing her pretty face. The hair had been red gold, the eyes blue and freckles in abundance spread across her cheeks nose and forehead. The young couple looked blissfully happy. Why should they not be, they were madly in love. She opened the jewellery box and took out the love letter which was almost worn out from the constant handling over so many years. As always, the wealth of emotion the words of this letter churned up never lessened. Though each and every word was so familiar, they were imprinted both in her mind and within her heart. The familiar silent tears slipped unchecked down the wrinkled skin of her now drooping cheeks. She unfolded the precious manuscript. Held it as carefully as if it were a priceless artefact. She smiled as the words of love warmed her poor heart.

3rd of June 1944

Dear Vera,

You can't imagine how much I miss you my love. Try not to worry, all members of the 8th Armoured Brigade including yours truly have arrived at our destination safe and sound. There is no cause to be alarmed if you don't hear from me for a while. Something big is on the horizon. I am not permitted to say anymore. All letters are screened as a security measure before posting. You must know how much I love you. All my dreams will come true the day that we are reunited. It is the thought of us spending the rest of our lives together, which enables me to bear the pain of our parting. Once the war is over we will make all our own dreams come true. We can visit all those places, which for now can only be dreamed of. I am certain that soon the war will be over. I just hope we will be the Victors in this war. It does not bear thinking of what would happen if the Germans should win. I keep your photo in the pocket nearest to my heart. The thought of your love gives me strength and keeps me warm in the cold hours of the night. I have so much to live for and that fills me with hope no matter what is in store. Please give my regards to your mother and father.

P.S You are my one true love there could never be anyone else. The first moment I set eyes on you the spark was lit and my love will go on burning bright for all eternity.

All my love always and forever

Teddy

xxxxxxxxxx

Vera folded the letter which had been repaired with clear sticky tape so many times. She placed it back in the jewellery box. She briefly held the engagement ring between finger and thumb, marvelling at the glitter of the solitaire diamond after all this time. Hot tears stung her eyes, she blinked them back but could do nothing about the constriction in her throat.

Such a long time to grieve but it never did become any easier to bear. She let the ring slip from her grasp. It was now suspended from the gold chain around her neck. It was time to go, Teddy would be waiting for her. She pulled on her woollen coat. Despite the warmth of the day she felt the cold keenly and shivered before pulling her scarf tighter around her throat.

It was a long walk to her destination. She stepped out of the front door and was delighted to feel the warmth of the sun on her face. The heat would ease the pain of her arthritic old bones. She felt ancient all of a sudden. Her footsteps slowed considerably the last few hundred yards.

At the cemetery gates she almost stumbled as her legs suddenly weakened. She struggled to make her way to the far eastern corner of the graveyard, a place she had visited more times than she could count. She could not stem the tide of tears from flowing as she walked to the area reserved for military graves. There were so many brass plaques on the wall. Right at the far end of the wall she stood still, in front of the polished memorial. Once again she read the inscription just as she had so many times before. Each time she mourned her own loss anew and that of everyone else who had suffered the pain of bereavement. Mr and Mrs Cartmell never did come to terms with the death of their only son. Within two years of his being killed they had both passed away. They had done one last thing for Teddy before they died. They had this plaque prepared and placed on the wall to commemorate the life and death of their beloved son.

So many lives cut short, so many hearts broken, so many tears shed. Enough sorrow to fill an ocean, for the families of men and women, who had paid the ultimate price for their loyalty to their fellow human beings. The inscription was poignant in its simplicity. A very few words to explain the heartache of a lost loved one. So much emotion in the two lines underneath the obituary.

In Loving Memory of our son Edward (Teddy) Cartmell

Born. January 31st 1925

Died. June 6th 1944. Normandy.

The tears flow without end.

Our hearts will never mend.

Mabel and Ted Cartmell.

The verse still rings true, my heart has never mended and I have shed a million tears. I still wait for Teddy, no-one else could ever have taken his place in my heart. I had the opportunity to marry. I was flattered by the proposals but it would not have been fair to accept. Any other man would have always been second best and no-one deserves that. All those lonely barren years, but none have been wasted. I had no child of my own but helped deliver so many into this world. Every baby briefly held in my arms was marvelled at. Each little miracle cuddled, before handing them over to the warm welcoming loving arms of their mothers.

I sink on to the bench and drift off to sleep in the sun. I must be dreaming and it's the most wonderful dream. A kiss on my lips wakes me and I relish the warmth and feeling of it as my eyes remain closed. Strong arms wrap around me in a tight embrace. The tenderness and joy of those strong arms fills me with the kind of happiness that I had long since forgotten. The arms that have held me unfold and I feel strength flow throughout my body and the aches and pains of old age are no more. I am filled with a light heartedness remembered from those long ago days of my youth. I have a wild urge to run and jump, to hop and skip, the way a young child would. At last I hear his voice and open my eyes to see the beloved face of Teddy.

'Vera my love now we can be together forever, I have waited so long for you.'

He stands before me smiling just the way I have always remembered, holding out his arms. I get up from the bench and run to him, then throw myself into his open arms. All the love held back for these past seventy years gushes forth, we kiss with all the passion of our youth. I have never known such happiness as this. I pull away a moment and turn to gaze at the old woman sat on the bench, who has mercifully died in her sleep. We link arms and walk away from the cemetery knowing we can wander all over this world, see all the places we have dreamed of and revel in this after life together for all eternity.

I wake up from the vivid dream and for many long drawn out seconds keep my eyes shut tight, revelling in the feeling of soaring high above the clouds. That same dream had been repeated many times, each one seemed more vividly real than the last. If I were to leave my bed right now I am certain that the secret of flight would be within my grasp. My thoughts are suddenly interrupted by a voice whispering in my ear. I listen intently but don't concern myself with who might be speaking to me.

'Don't open your eyes. Just listen to me and believe when I tell you, your wish for flight has been granted you have 24 hours starting from now!'

'Don't be so daft!' I call out.

I realise that my dream must still be ongoing but wonder who could have spoken to me. For some reason I have no thoughts as to who the whisperer might be and how they could have gained access to my bedroom. The voice is now silent and my eyes flicker open. Strange that I am fully conscious, the voice must have been a figment of my imagination.

Just for a fleeing moment I feel a surge of elation as my imagination runs away with me. What if my wish were granted? Just as quickly the thought is dismissed as the days tasks begin. I wash and get dressed; have some breakfast; then empty the washing machine of its load of wet laundry ready to hang on the line. I'm pegging out the last towel and suddenly feel buoyant. I had reached up towards the line to pull it down to my level. A quick glance at the ground fills me with excitement my feet are several inches from the ground.

'Oh wow, wow, wow, this is fantastic! My wish has been granted!'

I am unable to whistle, but would have done so if it had been at all possible. I quickly glance around to make sure no-one is watching. I have no wish to startle the neighbours.

I have a fervent question burning through my mind, which is quickly answered. As if by magic the voice whispers in my ear.

'The moment you rise above the ground you will be completely invisible to both humans and animals!'

The voice becomes silent once more. I take a huge leap and soar into the sky high above the houses. The higher my ascent the colder it feels. I descend quickly and walk back into the house. There is no time to waste. I emerge wearing my duffle coat, black boots, jeans and tartan wool scarf tied securely around my neck. I have a rucksack strapped to my back filled with essential items for my trip. I check to make sure both the front and back doors of my house are securely locked. It's a good job I won't be visible in the sky who would ever take a super human being seriously, while dressed in a duffle coat. A mental image of superman wearing a duffle coat over his tight fitting body suit tickles my funny bone and makes me laugh out loud. I have no intention of being anything like him, oh no! I am not wasting my precious twenty four hours of flying ability in the pursuit of saving humanity; knickers to that!

I have decided where I'm heading first of all. A quick trip to sunny Spain and an hour spent sunbathing, then paddling in the beautiful blue waters of the Mediterranean, a perfect start to the day. The speed of my flight is even faster than supersonic and just minutes later I arrive at my destination. I hastily unpack my rucksack. The towel is laid on the golden sand of the sun drenched beach and I have removed my outer clothes to reveal my shorts and cool cotton sun top. I pick up the bottle of sun factor 30 and rub the lotion vigorously into my arms, legs, face and neck. I put on my sunglasses and sunhat shielding my eyes from the glare of the sun. I revel at the heat of the warm sun rays on my pasty white skin. This is just fantastic, I think.... The train of thought is cut off abruptly by a loud scream.

I turn to see a woman further along the beach being mugged, by a massive, mean looking brute, his huge left fist has grabbed her handbag and he is just about to slap her with his right hand.

The basic instinct to offer help kicks in and a split second later I have grabbed a stick from the beach and hover above the mugger whacking him repeatedly on the top of his head. He loosens his grip on the handbag and looks up trying to protect his head from the stick raining blows down on it. He is amazed to find the stick just hovering in mid-air and decides to leg it full pelt along the beach. That will teach him, he might think twice before picking on another helpless victim. The woman overcome by shock sinks to the sand. I land a short distance behind her then approach her to ask if she is alright. The woman is a little dazed but assures me she is fine, and just grateful to have her bag safely within her grasp.

I pack my belongings into the rucksack, it's time to go. I'm not going to be able to relax here. Still it was great to have saved the woman from theft and assault. I stretch out my arms to the clear blue sky and soar straight up. I have my sunglasses firmly in place with a couple of bent hairclips. I love the sun but it's much too close now and the light is blinding.

I land smoothly in an alleyway in Rome, pop into a public convenience and emerge in a summer dress and sandals which had been packed carefully in my rucksack. The bag is a bit heavy with the weight of my duffle coat and boots plus other stuff I might need. I make my way to the nearest bench and sit down.

The architecture here in this beautiful city is spectacular. I am awed by such beautiful sumptuous surroundings. After half an hour I decide it's time to visit one of the most famous sights in the world and make my way to the Sistine Chapel. As I enter the building and try to find a quiet spot away from the crowds in order to take in the view of that most famous of ceilings ; a push from behind knocks me to the ground. Oh no, not another mugger I think.... My rucksack is still securely strapped on, but an angry man is chasing a thief shouting!

'Stop that man someone please, he's stolen my wallet!'

Oh bugger, I think! But I can't ignore the plea for help. Whoosh, I am up in the air and before the thief knows what's hit him I've aimed a swift kick at his backside and he keels over. The victim catches up grabs his wallet and other people come to his assistance, holding on to the thief until the police arrive.

Well I'm not going to get any peace here either; I realise. Oh well I have been to Rome, the Sistine Chapel is even more impressive than it looks in the brochures or on the television for that matter. Portugal is my next destination for a much deserved lunch, a plate of large prawns and a nice cool lager. Only the one though I am almost certain the drink driving laws extent to flight as well.

In a very short time I am sitting in a lovely restaurant with a plate of sizzling prawns and a tall slim glass of ice cold lager in my hand. Sweet dreams are made of this I think, tucking in to the wonderful lunch. I finish the meal and drink the refreshingly cold lager without incident. This is the first hour of the day so far when I've really been able to enjoy total contentment. I am full of gratitude for the gift of flight but so far it has been pretty tiring. Belting a mugger and kicking a thief in the backside has taken a great toll on my energy levels. I step out of the restaurant into the sunshine and wander through the streets of the small coastal fishing village, delighting in the peace and tranquillity of early afternoon. Where to next I wonder now that my batteries are recharged.

Before I know it the decision has already been made. I look down at the ruins of Pompeii amazed and delighted at the chance of this spectacular aerial view.

For a second my thoughts dwell on all those poor victims of the volcanic eruption so far back in the past. I pray for their souls in fervent hope that they are now at peace. I land once again on foreign soil and tag on to the end of a line of tourists following their guide. I stay for an hour and then head off to a new location.

The Eiffel tower looms into view. I never did fancy the thought of riding to the top in a lift, much too dangerous. That thought makes me giggle now there is nothing to fear. I fly right to the very top and land on a balcony out of plain sight from the other tourists, who are too busy taking in the surroundings to notice me. The view is spectacular as I knew it would be. I gaze around me taking in the awesome sight, imprinting it on to my memory. A woman screams loudly in distress!

'Help me please my child....'

The voice is cut off as the woman abruptly faints, overcome by the sheer terror of what has happened. Immediately I swoop down from the tower, this manoeuvre is both difficult and dangerous at great speed; for fear of crashing into the tower itself. I lunge and grab the terrified child just feet from the ground. She screams loudly in horror at the invisible arms holding her tight. Unable to quell the child's fear I hastily ascend and place her next to her mother's prone body. No-one notices right away, their concern concentrated on the prone body of the woman on the ground who is still unconscious. The child cries out.

'Mummy, wake up!'

The mother's eyes flutter open and she hugs the small body close sobbing loudly with relief. So much for not being a superhero I think to myself. The scene has brought tears to my eyes I hastily wipe them away. Super heroes don't cry, but then I am not one of them. I'm just an ordinary human being and a great softie at that.

I returned to my home filled with memories of this amazing day, though my limbs are aching. All this adventure is just so bloody exhausting.

Just before bedtime I'm unable to resist one last flight. My duffle coat is buttoned up, the tartan woollen scarf tightly wrapped around my neck. I pull up my hood and once more soar into the sky. The twinkling stars shine brighter the higher I rise above the ground. The sheer wonder and beauty of the world fills my heart with joy. I fly for hours and take in most of the sights across the length and breadth of the world.

At last I land in my own back garden, the place where this wonderful gift was realised. I watch the sun slowly rise into the sky signalling a brand new day. A day that dawns bright with promise. I feel the power slipping away like a cloak of silk slipping from my shoulders. What a great and most wonderful adventure this has been. It will live on in my memory until the very end of my life. I head indoors, now it's time to get some sleep and once more, sail away into the unconscious oceans filled with dreams.

I suppose for want of a better title you could describe me as a 'Ghostbuster'. Okay, I may not have a nuclear reacting machine strapped to my back. I don't wear a jump suit with a logo on the back. I don't own a converted ambulance and no, I don't live in a fire station house in New York City either. But the one undeniable talent I do possess is the ability not just too communicate, but to empathise with lost souls. I dislike the term 'medium', it sounds more like a dress size than a legitimate and honourable profession. On that thought a picture unfolded in my mind and made me giggle at the vivid scene evolving. A fully figured lady of quite generous proportions, let's pretend her name is Mrs Blossom, steps out of a changing room in a dress that doesn't quite fit. Her friend being a tactful person says.

'Marge the style of that dress and colour really do suit you, but I think it looks a little tight. Why not try a size larger, by the way what size is that?' Slightly red faced (Mrs Blossom) replies.

'Oh I think it's a medium.'

So you see, 'medium' to describe me is out of the question. Not being that keen on 'psychic' either, I much prefer the term 'spiritual adviser'.

I've just about finished painting and decorating my new premises, an office, small kitchenette and bathroom, positioned above a quaintly old fashioned tea room named 'The China Cup'. The proprietor has kindly offered to stock a number of my business cards on the counter. The rent of the rooms is not too exorbitant and I have enough funds for the next three months. Hopefully there will be plenty of work pouring in soon to enable my finances to grow steadily.

I have my own internet website set up, taken out two half page adverts in the local 'Mail & Gazette' and paid for a listing in Yellow Pages. To my reckoning every avenue is covered and my particular talent can be in no doubt because of previous testimonials from clients. Most of my previous clients have been recommended by word of mouth.

I've taken on these new premises just as a work place, so that my home can remain just that, a home. A place to relax in at the end of the working day and somewhere to switch off. Luckily for me I have the power to quite literally switch off my ability. My psychic power is on a par I imagine with radio frequency settings, minus the distortion of crackling sounds in between the set stations. All I have to do is imagine something like a light switch. I concentrate the mind on the off position of the switch for a couple of seconds and 'hey presto' no more spirits, no sounds of voices, just perfect peace and quiet.

The Telephone engineer interrupts my train of thought.

'All done now Mrs Smith the telephone and internet are connected. Good luck with the business whatever it entails. I must admit it does sound impressive though, 'spiritual adviser'. Don't believe in all that stuff myself though, if you don't mind me saying so! As far as I am concerned, if you can't see it then it doesn't exist and that's the way of it!'

'Thanks Fred glad to see everything is ready for me to get the business up and running. No offence taken about your own personal view of the existence or not of psychic ability. Everyone is entitled to their own opinion. I just hope there are plenty of potential clients out there. How about a cup of tea before you go and maybe I could throw in a chocolate biscuit or two?'

Ten minutes later Fred left after swallowing a large mug of tea and whole plate of biscuits. I was taking the mug to the sink in the small kitchenette when the phone rang. Hastily I picked up the phone pressed the green button introduced myself then listened carefully to the potential client on the other end of the line, jotted down a few details regarding name and location then soon the call ended. What a great start! Five minutes in business and already a client needing my help. I hugged myself happily.

Later that same afternoon I left the office and drove to Freckleton. It was easy to find the address thanks to the new Satnav in my car. I soon pulled up on the quiet side road in front of a neat bungalow. The front garden had a small square lawn with a border of marigolds along each edge. The garden was also surrounded by a short very neat picket fence painted white. A white wooden barred gate completed the garden and enclosed the front lawn.

I got out of the car, walked up to the front door and rapped the brass knocker lightly as it was quite noisy. Seconds later the door opened. The young woman who opened the door looked as though she had stepped straight out of the 1940's era. Her shining black hair was fashioned in a victory roll, her lips were painted in bright red lipstick and her dark arched eyebrows were pencilled in. Her face was powdered and there was a trace of mascara along thick lashes and black eye liner to finish the look. Her dress was of a floral pattern in subtle shades of blue. She wore navy blue patent leather peep toe, high heeled sling back shoes and her toenails and fingernails were painted in red lacquer a similar shade to her lips. She smiled broadly yet there was no sign of any joy in her eyes. There was a sadness about her that touched me deeply and my switch was hastily turned to the 'on' position. She introduced herself as Frances, giving no surname or any other information. She did offer me a cup of tea and I accepted graciously.

She led me into the living room decorated in the style befitting its owner. The overstuffed settee and armchairs, carpets, curtains, radio, light fitting, lamps and fireplace were all of the same 1940's era. There was nothing in the room to indicate that we could be living in the 21st century. I took a seat and gaged the surroundings. Frances left me alone and went to the kitchen to prepare the tea, returning just a few minutes later. She was holding a tray laden with the tea things and set it down on the coffee table in front of me. She poured tea into a china cup through a silver strainer to catch the leaves. Poured a little milk from the jug and added a spoon of sugar from the lidded sugar bowl. I stirred the tea after thanking her and took a sip, it was delicious. I was so used to the convenience of tea-bags nowadays, but remembered from childhood the taste of loose tea, so much more satisfying the taste seemed to me now.

'Mrs Smith I really do hope you can help me?'

'Of course I can help Frances, we both realise what needs to be done, so please don't worry. Sometimes departed souls get a little confused. It's understandable if a person has lived an extended life, with great age they have become weary. Their spirit reflects that weariness and they feel there is not enough energy to move on to the next stage. They remain trapped in a realm between this world and whatever awaits them in the next.'

Frances stared at me for a long time, sadness etched in the features of her lovely young face. She then turned her gaze towards the old fashioned clock in its wooden casing, set on the middle distance of the mantelpiece.

'I hoped Johnny would be back by now Mrs Smith I can't think where he could have got too.'

'It's alright I'm in no hurry Frances just tell me everything and I will be able to help you.'

'Ever since we moved in to this house there have been strange goings on. Inexplicable sounds can be heard in each and every room, even when they are empty. Each time I open a door and step into a room there is an abrupt and immediate silence. When I leave the room and close the door behind me the voices start to whisper at first, then become louder. I distinctly hear the sound of wheels rolling along wooden floorboards; there is a definite squeak as if the bearings are in need of a drop or two of oil to loosen them. Often there is music playing on the radio, it switches off and the music stops when I grasp the door handle and turn it. The only radio we own is in this living room. Each and every single night I hear voices whispering all around me. I'm so very frightened. I try to explain my fears to Johnny but he tells me there is nothing to worry about. I wish he were here with us now. I don't know what could have happened to him.'

The young woman is highly distressed and my empathy towards her is growing by the minute.

'Frances I assure you everything will be alright. Please don't worry. Just try to be calm, relax and close your eyes.'

She lowered her anxious body into the armchair and let her eyelids droop. Silent tears rolled down her cheeks tracing a path of wet black mascara smudges along the contours of her pretty face. The smooth creamy skinned brow furrowed deeply in anguish, her hands were clenched tight into tense fists. She appeared to slip easily into a trance like state, as soon as her eyes closed tightly. The butterfly wings of her fluttering eyelashes stopped beating and became still. Just seconds later the balled fists unclenched and transformed before my eyes. Dark brown mottled age spots appeared on her hands along with the deep wrinkles of an elderly woman. Her nails were ridged and discoloured. Her lovely dark hair turned to streaked white and grey, her face no longer young and pretty was still very attractive.

Despite the fact her features were deeply etched from the experiences gained throughout a long period of time. The, love, happiness, laughter, pure joy, plus the sadness, heartache, disappointment, grief and a myriad of other emotions failed to dispel completely the beauty of her youth.

The living room also went through a transformation before my eyes. The 1940's furniture slowly disappeared as if a magic wand had been waived. The room now contained   21st century design and latest technology, with the widescreen TV and Digi- box. The window blinds were metallic silver, the geometric patterned carpet monochrome, to match the black leather sofa and a modern fireplace with pebbles instead of coal behind the smoked glass. Twin chrome and black uplighter standard lamps and wallpaper in silver and grey completed the ultra - modern style.

An elderly man with snow white hair entered the room with footsteps barely audible. His faded blue eyes registered so much joyfulness as his gaze rested on Frances' lovely face. The love inside him so evident I could feel the power of it deep inside. He turned his head in my direction, a bright smile curved his lips upwards at the corners, he uttered just one word with so much emotion it spoke volumes.

'Thanks.'

He leaned in close to Frances and whispered her name. Her eyelids fluttered like delicate gossamer wings and she gazed deeply into his eyes, joy radiating from her whole being. Holding her hands in his he helped her out of the chair and on to her feet. They stood a little apart for long seconds just staring into each other's eyes. No words were needed. They had found each other again. They had been lost, but now thankfully reunited. My task was now completed.

The elderly couple embraced each other and their lips met in a brief but tender kiss. They turned one last time towards me and waved goodbye before fading from sight.

I checked my watch registering the fact only thirty minutes had passed since I entered the room and yet it seemed like hours. I heard the key turn in the front door lock and a young couple stepped into the hall. They warily popped their heads around the living room door but stayed put in the safety of the hall. Each of them wore the same expression of trepidation as they gazed inside the room and seemed to be listening intently. I beamed a warm smile and gestured for them to come inside.

'Everything is fine now, the house is all yours. There won't be any more incidents. All is quiet and peaceful. The lost soul that remained here has finally found her way home.'

They thanked me with genuine gratitude and offered me a cup of tea. I politely declined, after sinking a full pot over the last half. I left their house feeling content and optimistic that my new venture would be a great success.

The excruciating ordeal of silence maintained throughout dinner was now mercifully over. Both boys had left the table without uttering a single word. Emily experienced the familiar tightening in her chest and the heat of unshed tears threatening to flow free. She knew they were now in hiding close by, eagerly awaiting her reaction. She was determined not to succumb to tears; they would enjoy seeing her cry; she was not going to give them the satisfaction of witnessing weakness of any kind.

How many more meals where the boys played deaf and dumb would she have to endure, in the company of her twin step sons? It just didn't bear thinking about. It had been only two short years since she first met their father Harry, yet it seemed a lifetime ago.

Harry's first wife Sarah had died giving birth to their twin boys. She suffered a sudden escalation in blood pressure which caused a massive heart attack. Harry's overwhelming grief over the loss of his beloved wife had at that time; threatened to push him over the edge and into a complete mental breakdown. Initially he transferred all blame for their mother's death on to their baby sons Andy and Mark. Both his state of mind and abject sorrow resulted in total rejection of the two tiny infants.

Both sets of parents, Harry's and Sarah's took on the joint responsibility of caring for their grandsons. This obligation allowed each one of them to deal with the sudden and unexpected bereavement; by pouring all their energies into caring for their newly born grandchildren. It was a heart wrenching, devastatingly sorrowful time for Sarah's parents, as they mourned the death of their only child, while caring for her beloved babies. That the baby boys resembled their mother so closely in looks was both a great comfort but also a sad and constant reminder of their own great loss.

The certain knowledge that some small part of their daughter now lived on in these tiny babies was all the reason they needed to carry on now, with the sometimes arduous task of living.

The babies were almost a year old before Harry began to finally take some interest in his infant sons. Since the death of his beloved wife, he had concentrated all surplus energy into furthering his career and worked every hour possible. He still hadn't been able to properly deal with the intensely raw emotion of bereavement, it was locked deep inside his heart. A heart encased in a barrier he had built.

One particular evening he returned from work much later than usual. As he entered the hall there was the sound of voices, in animated conversation between his parents and in-laws in the living room. The subject up for discussion was his role as a father or lack of it. His own father spoke in a voice both passionate and determined.

'It's about time Harry started to shoulder some of the responsibility for those two babies of his!'

'I agree with you about that my love but how will he manage to care for them? After all he is our son, we can't let him down when he needs us so much?' His mother's tone of voice filled with raw emotion.

'After relying on us to take care of them for so long; it breaks my heart that Harry acts as if those little angels don't even exist. My poor Sarah would have given them all the love in the world if only she had been given the chance.' His mother-in-law sobbed.

'Now, now, don't upset yourself, please don't start crying again love, it does you no good. I am grieving for the loss of our daughter just as much as you are. None of us wants to fall out with Harry but this situation can't carry on as it is indefinitely. The babies are his responsibility, his flesh and blood. He is their father and should be taking an interest in their well- being. It's high time he started to acknowledge the fact they are his children and at the very least, make an offer to help with the care of them.' He placed a comforting arm around the heaving shoulders of his sobbing wife.   Harry didn't wait to hear anymore, he just slipped quietly upstairs, and for the first time since they arrived home from the maternity hospital walked into the nursery. He opened the blue and white teddy bear patterned curtains, enabling the room to flood with the light of a full silvery moon. He gazed down in fascination at the perfectly formed baby boys that were his and Sarah's sons. As he gazed into the cots the nightlight seemed to cast a golden glow onto the plump pink baby cheeks of the sleeping infants. Their bright blonde hair and long dark lashes they had inherited from their mother. It seemed to him as though he were gazing down on angels they looked so perfect. Hesitantly he leaned over the cots and very lightly caressed their little cheeks with his forefinger. The warmth of soft velvet skin permeated the barrier of ice encasing his heart. Little by little the ice cracked in tiny fractures until the force of emotion hit home and melted the remainder.

The floodgates opened as hot tears welled up behind his lowered lids forming puddles which overflowed spilling onto his cheeks. Harry's shoulders heaved as the great racking sobs brought forth a torrent of emotion draining away all the bitterness held inside.

When his anger and bitterness were finally poured out, the emptiness was replaced by an overwhelming and powerful feeling so strong the force of which he had long forgotten. Like the shock of an electricity bolt to the brain he felt the one emotion which had been long neglected. Pure, simple love, weaved a course along his veins and arteries followed quickly by a surge of pride and a powerful instinct to protect these small scraps of humanity from any danger known or unforeseen. Suddenly he could not wait for the eyelashes to flutter open and these little beings to awake. He picked up each baby as if they were constructed of fine porcelain. With a son cradled in each of his arms he made his way down the stairs.

The voices ceased immediately as Harry entered the room with both sons cradled lovingly and surprisingly still asleep in his arms. A beaming smile was soon mirrored on the faces of both his own parents and Sarah's. There was no need for words as they hugged each other. Emotion like fireworks sparked and crackled and for the first time in almost a year they were finally reunited as a family.

Both grandmothers gently removed the sleeping babies from their father's arms and took them back to the nursery, placing them gently back in their cots and tucking the blankets around their small bodies. When the women left the room they hugged each other with tears streaming down their cheeks. After a long time they broke apart and smiled warmly knowing that their roles in the babies' lives would change after tonight. Harry had much to learn about childcare but they would gladly teach him the basics help him out whenever needed, but also take a step back, after all was said and done he was the babies' father.

The next day Harry decided it was now time to sort out all his dead wife's possessions with the help of his two mothers. The only thing he kept apart from photo albums, was her engagement ring, there was too much sentiment attached to that particular object and he couldn't bear to part with it.

Four years on things seemed so much easier, the boys were now in school. With the help of his family and in-laws he could once more concentrate on his career. He had mainly worked from home over the previous few years, to make up for the time he had neglected the children in their babyhood. He had in fact spoiled the children absolutely rotten. Despite several pleas from both grandmothers, to put a stop to constantly overindulging the children, their concerns fell on deaf ears. In part as a consequence, both Andy and Mark though no less angelic looks wise, were in fact a pair of spoiled, nasty, spiteful little boys. It wasn't just about the material things they had gained, despite the fact everything they had demanded they got. They had been showered with love and affection from their father and both sets of grandparents, yet there was something inside of them which was both cold, dark and totally inexplicable.

Harry didn't seem to notice that they were friendless. He never speculated as to why they were never invited to birthday parties or asked to other children's houses to play. They were never asked to join after school activities. Every time he went to pick them up from school no other child walked within yards of his two sons'.

Both sets of grandparents were extremely worried about the boy's behaviour and had been for some time. Neither one of them wanted to approach Harry and disclose their own fears about the boys' true natures. After all he was a lonely widower and did his best (or so he thought) for his children.

Increasingly the grandparents withdrew their offers of regular babysitting. The boys after school childcare was attended to without question, but once their duty was done and Harry came home, he was quickly left alone with his sons.

When the boys were six years old Harry had to go away for a weekend to attend a seminar in Brighton. Both sets of grandparents moved in to the house to care for the boys during his absence. Harry was grateful for their help but puzzled by the fact that they all intended to stay.

'I can't understand why it will take all four grandparents to care for the boys, though it is much appreciated. After all they are never any trouble!'

'Look Harry none of us are getting any younger and the boys can be a real handful when you are out of the house. It is either all of us staying or you will have to get someone else to babysit!'

Harry was surprised at the venomous tone in his mother's voice but declined to make a comment. He didn't give the outburst a seconds thought after he left the house.

Much later, on arrival at the Hotel he noticed a young woman struggling to carry a very large suitcase up the steps to the entrance.

'Please let me help you with that, you have packed everything plus the kitchen sink I take it?'

He was surprised to find himself smiling and felt warmed when it was returned it with one of gratitude and relief.

'Thanks, I have never been to one of these seminars before and couldn't make up my mind what to pack so have brought almost everything I own.'

Her eyes were alight as the corners of her mouth lifted into a full on genuine beaming smile.

After checking in they went their separate ways. Later that same day they were both surprised and pleased to find themselves wearing name badges with the same company logo.

'Hello Emily what's a nice girl like you doing in a place like this?' Harry laughed embarrassed at the corny old line. But could think of nothing else to say.

'Pleased to meet you Harry, what makes you think I'm nice?' Emily giggled.

By the end of the weekend it was as if they had known each other for years. They talked and laughed with the ease of great friends but there was a spark of something more. As luck would have it they both lived in the same town but worked in different branches of the company.

Six months later Harry got the family together for a small party to introduce Emily. Both his parents and in-laws took an instant liking to her, they were charmed by the young woman. She was possessed of genuine warmth and chatted easily to the family, fitting in right away. With her dark wavy hair, skin a shade of pale cream, emerald green eyes, and pretty features she really was lovely. Though she was the complete opposite of his wife in looks and personality, he could not help himself falling in love with her. Harry detected a slight detachment from both Andy and Mark but seemed totally blinded by the true nature of his sons.

His mother still shuddered at the memory of finding both boys in the shed at the bottom of the garden. She had walked in unannounced and was deeply shocked and sickened at the boys' behaviour. With lighted candles they were cruelly burning the legs off a poor defenceless spider. She had been so angry, the candles were violently wrenched away and she slapped their hands much harder than intended. After that particular episode she spent even less time in their company. Harry brushed off the incident, with a boys will be boys' attitude. As far as he was concerned they were perfect and could not possibly do anything wrong.

Now Emily and Harry had been married for just over a year, but almost from day one she had soon realised what little horrors her step sons really were. In the company of their father they put on Oscar winning performances as the most perfectly obedient children. When Harry was out of the way, they played the utmost cruel tricks conceivable. Only this morning she had inhaled the most horrible stench in the boy's room when she went to collect their laundry. There was a dirty stained sweatshirt lying on the floor half under the bed. As she bent to pick it up, she reeled in horror as the long bald tale of a large black rat followed by its putrid corpse slid from the scrunched up shirt. Bile rose up in her throat and she ran to the bathroom feeling sick and shaking. Revulsion filled her lungs with a dark stinking substance.

'Mark, Andy, come here this minute you boys are cruel and revolting. Your father is going to hear about this believe me!'

Manic laughter filled the house and the boys ran out from their room, the poor dead rat corpse hanging from Mark's hand. He waived it in her face in a taunting manner. She recoiled in horror and ran down the stairs headed in to the lounge and closed the door before phoning her mother-in-law begging her to come round to the house. Ten minutes later their grandmother's car pulled up outside in the drive and on opening the door, Emily ran into her arms tears staining her face. The boys were reprimanded severely by their grandmother but they were far from stupid. Amidst the chaos of earlier they had somehow left the house unseen and disposed of the rat's putrid corpse.

Emily had once again been made to feel like the invisible woman during dinner. Neither of the boys spoke a word or even acknowledged her existence. As she stacked the empty plates to take to the kitchen surprisingly both boys approached and as one said.

'Let us help you Emily we'll empty the table for you and dry the dishes after the washing up is done.'

She eyed them with suspicion but decided to accept the offer of help despite their voices sounding robotic and totally devoid of emotion.

'Okay then let's get on with it. Harry will be home soon. Don't try anything funny and just to let you know this won't let you off the hook. That was a nasty spiteful trick you pair played earlier, and your father is not going to be able to ignore what you have done this time.'

For the next 20 minutes peace reigned and the kitchen was soon cleared of dirty dishes and pots. While Emily washed up the boys dried each item and put them away in the cupboards. Why can't they always be like this, she thought? I would like nothing better than to care for them. The truth is they scare the wits out of me, she reluctantly admitted to herself and involuntarily shuddered.

Harry arrived home minutes later and before Emily could speak he recognised the look on her face and the signs of anger instantly registered on his features.

'Don't tell me my sons have upset you again, what is it this time?' Emily felt the force of his anger like a sharp slap across the face. Instead of telling him of the horrible incident of that morning, knowing he would take their side over hers, she astounded him by singing their praises.

'Harry no need to be so defensive I wanted to let you know the boys have helped me this evening clearing the table and drying dishes. They did a first class job.'

The anger instantly melted away softening the frown lines of his handsome face. A slow smile lifted the corners of his mouth. He was heartily sick and tired of having to hear Emily's constant complaints about his sons. Unknown to him the boys directed their cold eyed stares towards their stepmother. They then turned to stare at each other with a horrible knowing smile mirrored on each face. Emily went in to the kitchen and prepared Harry's evening meal. He went upstairs for a shower and the boys ran up the stairs to their bedroom. Just a few minutes later the table was re-set. A bottle of wine and two glasses placed on the pristine white tablecloth. The minute Harry entered the dining room, Emily placed the dinner plate on the table with a warning that it was still hot from the oven. Harry put a forkful of food into his mouth.

Upstairs in their bedroom the boys stopped what they were doing and crept silently onto the landing listening intently. They were quickly rewarded by the sound of angry shouts from their father.

'Emily. What the hell is happening here?'

'What's wrong?'

'I very nearly choked on this ring.'

He used a napkin to clean the food from the ring and on recognition a dark raging anger welled up inside him and he shouted at Emily.

'What is Sarah's engagement ring doing on my plate? Why would you take it from my drawer? Don't you have enough of your own jewellery? This ring is all I have left of my wife; that and our sons. Now I understand why you are always complaining about them. You are always trying to convince me that they are some kind of delinquents. All this time the answer has been staring me in the face. You are   jealous, jealous of a dead woman!'

'Believe me I haven't the faintest idea how the ring got there. I would never dream of touching anything which belonged to you, or Sarah or anyone else for that matter. How you could accuse me of something so dreadful as stealing, not to mention making up stories of the boy's bad behaviour let alone the jealousy, it's just beyond me. You are blind to your sons, they are truly evil. If you have any doubts on that score then you have to know about the vile trick they pulled today, just phone your mother. I really have had just about enough!'

Emily grabbed her coat, bag and car keys then slammed the front door with great and deliberate force on her way out.

Some hours later a taxi pulled up outside Harry's house and he ran outside just in time to pay the fare and open the car door for his wife. He gathered her into his arms and this time he told her how sorry he was for everything. His mother and father appeared in the hallway behind him along with the boy's other set of grandparents. Emily was unusually more than a bit tipsy after downing several large glasses of wine, but then it was not unusual given what she had recently endured. Explanations could wait until tomorrow, right now she desperately needed sleep.

The next morning the family assembled in the living room minus Mark and Andy. Harry was astonished and deeply ashamed that his indulgence and lack of any discipline had led to his sons becoming such thoroughly nasty young boys. During   the previous night he'd listened with mounting horror of the spiteful and cruel deeds his own children had committed. He had been completely deluded, automatically believing his sons could do no wrong. His mother had even related the fact both boys had faked illness trying to get her to believe Emily was trying to poison them. They would have done anything to get rid of her. It was more than a little late but not too late he hoped, to teach some discipline and steer his boys on to the right track. Surely it was not too late for that. They could not be all bad, could they? Unknown to their father the boys were in the garden crouching under the open window, listening intently to every single word that was spoken in the room.

'No father, we are not all bad. Not just yet; but we are working on it!' They whispered the words, then suddenly started to laugh; louder and louder. The sound of which was both humourless and unnerving!

Jean was in a brilliant frame of mind, as she eagerly ran to answer the ringing phone. She had the show to look forward to. The anticipation of actually going to see Paul Mackenzie live on stage had kept her smile firmly in place since the day she purchased the tickets! The look of contentment plastered on her face soon faded as she listened to the voice of the caller on the other end of the line.

'Hello Jean I know it's short notice love and I apologise but our Jimmy is really very ill, coughing non-stop, vomiting incessantly and his forehead is so hot you could fry bacon on it. Frank will drop off the ticket later on the way back from A&E. We have to go right away Jean it's bound to be a very long wait and we are so worried. So sorry for letting you down. I was so looking forward to seeing the show with you!'

'Look Lily it's not your fault love. You must both be worried sick. I hope Jimmy will be alright, let me know how he is when he's seen the Doctor. Bye for now, best of luck.'

Disappointment like a lead weight caused her shoulders to slump in defeat she had being dying to see the show for ages. It was very doubtful she could get anyone else to take the second ticket at this late period. The tickets they had purchased was for the performance tomorrow night. Just as the thought entered her mind she heard a rap on the living room door and her son Jack popped his head around it, a beaming smile on his handsome face as always.

'Hello mum why are you looking so glum, you look like you've swallowed a wasp or something?'

'I'm so disappointed because of Lily, she just phoned to let me know she can't go to the show tomorrow night. It's not her fault though, poor Jimmy has suddenly taken very ill to-day. Her and Frank are so worried they have taken him to the A&E Department at the hospital. I have been so excited for weeks at the thought of going to see that show Jack. Where am I going to find someone else to go with me at such short notice?'

'What time does it start tomorrow evening mum?'

'The show starts at 7 o'clock and finishes at 9.30. I don't suppose you know of anyone who might be interested in going? The tickets are paid for and I would rather someone else used the spare one than lose out on both.'

'Well if it wouldn't be too embarrassing to be seen out with your favourite son, then I wouldn't mind going with you. I don't have anything planned for tomorrow evening and I know how much you have looked forward to going.'

'Oh that would be just brilliant love. What did I do to deserve such a wonderful son?'

They both laughed at that and hugged each other tightly for a few seconds.

'That is a date then mum!'

Jean wondered for the umpteenth time why Jack had not yet found (The One). He was a tall, slim, good looking young man. Okay so she was prejudiced, after all he was her only son. But then she wasn't the only one to agree that he was also kind, thoughtful, hard- working and great company to be with. When he smiled it lit up the room. Every smile was perfectly matched with a warm twinkling in his eyes. He possessed a ready and brilliant wit and was always eager to offer a helping hand to anyone in need. Since Nick's death it had just been the two of them, but she didn't want him to feel obliged to take the responsibility for her well-being. He was young and had a life of his own to get on with.

At 25 years old he had been ready to move into a flat of his own when tragedy struck. Nick was driving to the flat with some boxes when a lorry veered out of control and crashed into the drivers' side of his car. According to the Police and Ambulance crew he'd died instantly on impact and would not have suffered any pain. Jack had insisted on staying with her until she could cope alone and twelve months on he was still living at home.

Jean would miss him terribly when he eventually did move out, but he needed to go as soon as he could. She had to make him see it was time to put himself first, he must take the opportunity to live his own life to the full. In Jean's train of thought that meant finding true love and happiness with Miss Right and enjoying the rest of their lives together. She may be a widow, but she still had memories of the great love her and Nick shared, she wanted her beloved son to find that kind of love for himself. She was ever the romantic at heart.

The very next evening Jean and Jack joined the long queue outside the theatre. Even though they had pre-booked and had their tickets, the box office was snowed under on this first opening night. Jean had often dreamed of seeing Paul Mackenzie after watching the television series some years previously. She was convinced it would be impossible for anyone to hypnotise her, but did wonder briefly if Jack may be a bit more susceptible.

One hour into the show Paul Mackenzie asked for two volunteers, specifically a man and woman in their mid-twenties. Jack had no intention of raising his hand but Jean had other ideas, so to please her he waived his arm in the air and was summoned to the stage while the audience applauded excitedly. As he walked towards the stage he had the chance to glance before him the view of a pair of very shapely legs. He raised his eyes a little further and admired the young woman's stunning figure. The back view was very impressive right up to the long auburn hair cascading across her shoulders in glossy waves. As he followed her on to the stage he was awestruck at the sight of bright blue eyes and pretty features. She gave him a smile full of warmth and friendliness, he was instantly hooked. He returned her smile and they were seated side by side on high stools facing the audience.

Both of them experienced a sudden attack of nerves as they noticed for the first time an audience filled with hundreds of faces staring back at them. Instinctively for a brief moment they clasped hands and the audience cheered loudly and whistled as they saw the obvious spark of attraction between the young people.

Paul addressed the audience and commanded that they remain silent during the routine and order was instantly restored. You could hear a pin drop, the silence was unnatural in a place filled with so many people. Paul approached Jack first and then told him that on the count of five he should close his eyes and wait for instructions. He then turned his attention towards Jane and repeated the same words. A loud short drum roll was the signal to put his subjects in to a trance. In turn he approached both Jack and Jane, he was amazed at the susceptibility of these two young people to the power of suggestion. They were hypnotised into a trance almost instantaneously. From where Jean sat she was convinced it was totally genuine but that didn't stop her experiencing a twinge of guilt for urging Jack to volunteer. She fervently hoped that nothing embarrassing would happen, instinctively she crossed her first two fingers on each hand.

Paul dipped his hand in to the right hand pocket of his jacket and took out some round objects. He held up three shiny green buttons to show the audience then gave the order for them to remain completely silent. He spoke to Jack first saying.

'Jack can you hear me?'

'Yes Paul I can.'

'I am going to count to five and when you open your eyes you will take off your watch and hand it over to me. In exchange for your watch I will give you three gold coins.'

'1,2,3,4,5'

Instantaneously Jack's eyes fluttered open and he loosened the strap of his watch and took it off. Paul held up the buttons once more for the audience to see. He then counted them out one by one and placed them in Jack's hand. Jack handed over the watch and gazed at the buttons with a big smile on his face as he thought what a great bargain he'd struck, these gold coins must be worth a fortune. Paul snapped his fingers and Jack's eyes felt suddenly leaden and his lids fell quickly like a pair of shutters. Now it was Jane's turn.

'Jane can you hear me?'

'Yes Paul, I can.'

'On the count of five you will open your eyes to find yourself standing behind a counter sorting watches in a display case. A customer will enter the shop and try to buy a watch with three green buttons. You will have to deal with the situation.'

Immediately Jane rose from her stool and stood behind the imaginary counter arranging the invisible watches in the display case. Paul handed her Jack's watch and she took it without a word.

'Jack when you wake on the count of five you will enter a shop and buy a new watch with the gold coins. 1,2,3,4,5.'

Jack's eyes fluttered open and he made straight for Jane's counter, he stood staring at the watches in the imaginary display case. He pointed to the one she was holding and asked the price of it. She told him and he held out the buttons. Jane looked at the shiny green buttons and burst into laughter.

'You have to be joking if you think these will be worth the price of that watch. I will accept cash or credit card but not three green buttons!'

Jack looked confused all he could see were the gold coins in his hand she must be winding him up.

'These gold coins must be worth a small fortune, definitely more than enough to pay for that watch!'

The audience had started to giggle at first, then it soon escalated to loud laughter. Jean wondered briefly what would happen next, her guilt at forcing Jack to volunteer increased by the minute, her face flushed scarlet with a mixture of both trepidation and a slight sense of embarrassment. The scene being played out on stage had the audience hooked. Paul couldn't believe how well the trick was working and marvelled at the subjects he had hypnotised. Jane and Jack were haggling across the imaginary counter. All of a sudden they stopped talking and stared at each other. Jane smiled at Jack and her eyes lit up as she said.

'Look if you really want the watch that much I am sure we can come to some sort of arrangement, how about a small deposit?'

Paul was astounded at the chemistry between the couple. Like static electricity you could almost hear it crackle. He'd had a great reaction from the audience, much more than he could have hoped for. It was now time to end the show on a high note.

As Jack and Jane left the stage hand in hand there was thunderous applause from the audience. They had already arranged a date for the following evening. Jean looked on with a warm feeling in her heart and a smile on her face. Her guilty feelings disappeared at once and were replaced by hope and sheer joy, the young couple appeared to her to be made for each other.

Six months later Jack and Jane bounded through the living room door like a pair of excited children. Jean recognised that look as the one she had once shared with Nick not so   long ago. The announcement was no surprise but no less welcome for that. She rose from the settee and held on to Jane's left hand while admiring the glittering diamond engagement ring decorating the third finger. She hugged her son first, then Jane with so much love and happiness. Then she stood back to gaze at this lovely couple, her heart filled with emotion. If only Nick were here to share this moment! She sensed the familiar build- up of unshed tears prick the back of her eyes, but was determined not to let them escape. Despite the brief aching inside her heart for Nick's lost love, her overall joy for the young couple was genuine. If they experienced a tenth of the love and happiness she had enjoyed in her 30 year marriage to Nick, then their lives together would be wonderful indeed. She was gaining an already much loved future daughter-in-law. How much life had changed for the better over these past six months! There was so much to look forward to now, first the wedding and in the future maybe a grandchild or two. Later as she told her friend Lily the good news over the phone she ended the conversation with the words.

'I couldn't believe that three green buttons could have been responsible for all that!'

Handbag

That particular morning I awoke, relieved to escape the clutches of a dream which enfolded me in a cold blanket of fear. Perspiration like tiny glass beads clung to my brow and danced among the roots of my hair, until the sticky warm droplets slid down my cheeks and soaked the neckline of my blue cotton pyjama jacket. The only aspect of the dream which remained vivid in my mind, was the image of a distinctive old fashioned handbag displayed in the front window of an Oxfam shop. Why the memory of this seemingly ordinary object sent shivers hurtling along the length of my spine, was a mystery to me at that moment. Yet the very sight of it imprinted to mind left me cold, as if my shoulders were encased in a mantle of dread.

Was it just curiosity; or the guiding finger of fate that led me to drive into town a couple of hours later that same morning? Sometimes there are no rational explanations for the paths we take or plans we set in motion. All I know with certainty is that the compulsion to act immediately was so persuasive, it would have been impossible to ignore it!

After parking the car on the outskirts of town, I headed towards the shops after   crossing the main road which leads to its centre. The Bus Station was directly in front of me   so I glanced up at the clock tower to check the time. Just a few metres further ahead, the   Oxfam shop was situated on a corner of two adjoining streets.

Logic attempted to warn me that a dream or nightmare is just part of the subconscious mind and can't possibly have any bearing on events that happen in the real world. Our brains process a vast mine of information collected each day. This data is relegated in varying degrees to each of the numerous files held in deep recesses of the mind according to their importance. Dreams are the thoughts and impressions which have not been properly filed away in to the relevant groups. These thoughts and impressions are left   unchecked, allowing them to dance wildly and at random, across the wide screen of the subconscious. This spectacle is similar to viewing a feature film where the scenes are haphazard and shown out of sequence.

My footsteps had deliberately slowed down the pace, as anxiety set in the closer I drew towards my destination. Then before too long there it was just ahead. The short distance had been paced and I came to a standstill on the pavement facing the Oxfam shop. Ridiculous though it sounds, the fingers were interlaced tightly on both my right and left hands. My lowered gaze was lifted slowly from ground level until the view was directly in line with the window display. I exhaled loudly with pure relief to find that the handbag featured in my dream was not in plain sight. Suddenly my actions were beyond my control. I could move neither backwards or forwards, but felt an unseen force compel me to step through the door and into the shop. It was as if I were being pushed from behind by invisible hands.

Just inside the entrance my eyes were automatically drawn to the glass shelf of a display cabinet along the far wall. Lined up along the shelf there stood a selection of bags in various styles and colours. As one in particular caught my eye, ice cold tremors traced a path from the base of my spine to the top of my head, causing an involuntary shudder. The icy sliver of shock caused tendrils of hair to stand upright from my scalp. The sensation was akin to a bolt of electricity shooting through me. The sight before me in prominent position on the glass shelf was the distinctive handbag I vividly remembered from my dream. The old fashioned Gladstone bag of cream coloured woven straw, the brown leather double rolled handles and a metallic buckle fastener. My legs became suddenly unstable, threatened to collapse beneath me. I found myself stumbling uncertainly nearly falling to the floor. Time seemed to slow down until I became aware of someone patting my hand in a soothing motion.

'Are you alright my dear should I call for a Doctor?'

I glanced up and caught sight of eyes the colour of melted dark chocolate. The brown eyed woman with curly black hair gave me a look of warmth and genuine compassion. I found my voice just then.

'There is no need to call for a Doctor. I have suffered a bit of a shock that's all. I really am fine. How embarrassing this is! I do thank you for your concern though, it's much appreciated.'

To my surprise the lady handed me a plastic carrier containing a handbag. Having no recollection whatsoever of purchasing it, but not wishing to make a fuss to add further to my embarrassment, I once more thanked her for her concern before beating a hasty retreat from the shop. My face flushed scarlet, I could not get away fast enough. Once outside I inhaled deeply filling my lungs with fresh air, after an unwelcome and unexpected feeling of exhaustion. I walked straight to the car park and drove home.

On arrival at my home the carrier containing the handbag was pushed far from sight in to the wardrobe of my spare bedroom. Though it remained out of sight it was not out of mind and my thoughts were continuously drawn to it like metal to a strong magnet. If only I had someone to confide in. I was used to living alone and in the main quite content, but on occasion it would have been good to have some company.

Later that same evening a burning curiosity cast away any former doubts. I came to the decision it would be safe to take a look at the handbag. I retrieved the carrier from the wardrobe and hesitated only for a split second before pulling the handbag free. The instant my fingers came in contact with the leather handles a slight quiver pulsed through the tips of my fingers and ran along the length of both my arms. It was like a power surge of pure heat. The shock of the sensation made me drop the handbag to the floor, before reluctantly picking it up and placing it back inside the carrier. I opened the wardrobe door, and literally threw the carrier as far to the back of the shelf as possible so it was no longer in sight. The conscious decision was made there and then to donate the handbag first thing the next morning to another charity shop.

That night I drifted along the path of sleep and into the same dream from the previous night. The one exception being that another element of the story was revealed. An elderly lady appeared before me to stand at the foot of my bed. Her curly white hair neatly styled, her pale almost opaque blue eyes and rosy cheeks were as real to me as any other person I had ever seen. The lady was small of stature, slightly rotund but her posture was perfect, she stood straight backed head held high. I remember vividly her clothes the cream mohair coat with a lilac flower petal broach pinned to the right lapel. The blouse she wore was of a cream silk material, her shoes were two-tone brown and cream leather. All this detail I noted until it came to the bag draped casually over her arm.

Shock jolted me from the realms of sleep my eyes fluttered open, a trembling hand reached desperately for the bedside lamp switch. My hair now damp clung to my head, sweat glistened, beads of moisture trickled down my face in several rivulets. The skin on my back seemingly crawled like an infestation. I leapt from the bed as if escaping an attacker. I ran to the bathroom and took a long hot shower. I dressed in clean clothes and the remainder of that night was spent in the sitting room. All the lights were switched on to flood the room and banish any dark corners. There I sat eagerly awaiting the first light of dawn.

The next day life carried on as normal while I went about my daily routine. I tried desperately to push away any memory of the vivid dream, or nightmare as I came to realise it. Curiously I had managed to put thoughts of the handbag aside; for some unfathomable reason it remained inside the carrier on the shelf in my wardrobe. I left it there reluctant to touch even the carrier after the shock of what happened the previous evening.

The dream was repeated that very night and unfolded once more with the same familiarity plus one additional aspect. This time during the re-run of the dream scene the elderly lady walked slowly forwards and stood facing me at the end of my bed. She stared deep into my eyes her gaze boring into me with the intensity of longing! I had no idea what it could be she longed for, but understood all too well her helplessness. Sadness welled up inside me in such abundance, it stirred a wealth of emotion as powerful as her gaze. Long after I awoke the sadness clung on and left me feeling cold and despondent.

The next night aspects of the dream were played out before me in all too memorable scenes, much as an old recognisable film reel rolling along. The lady walked towards my bed her footsteps silent. Once facing me she stood still, gazed deep into my eyes and her lips moved slowly, the voice softly whispered the pleading words.

'Harriet help me please!'

Night after night the dream held me in its thrall. There was to be no escape from the repeated and familiar ritual it had now become. Gradually though my fear had lessened considerably as an awareness gained clarity. The only way for me to have any peace of mind was to carry out my own investigation. Gather all possible facts that could be collected about this poor lost soul who haunted my sleep every single night. It seemed entirely plausible this lady haunting my dreams was also once the owner of the distinctive handbag lying on a shelf in my wardrobe. There was now no doubt in my mind that she needed my help. As yet I didn't know how it was possible to give that help or even what it might involve.

It had been a whole month since I had received the nasty shocks from the bag and flung it unceremoniously out of sight; though definitely not out of mind. Now I decided it was time to retrieve the handbag and investigate the contents, if in fact; there were any. I walked with purpose to the spare bedroom and once there, made my approach to the wardrobe with purposely slow footsteps.

With some trepidation I turned the handle and opened the door, all was silent within. I retrieved the carrier from its hiding place at the back of the top shelf. I walked downstairs to my living room and sat on the settee hesitating for just a moment. I then pulled the bag carefully from its plastic carrier and examined the exterior in minute detail. Whatever it was that caused the series of shocks the last time I handled the bag had now been drained away. The power source had somehow inexplicably been deactivated. For a long while I held the bag in my hands. I was reluctant to open it for fear of what lay within which might escape and cause untold mayhem.

With slow deliberate movements I unfastened the buckle, freed the clasp and opened the bag, before gazing inside with caution. A long slow sigh of relief escaped my lips on realisation that the bag appeared at first glance to be empty. There was nothing remotely sinister lying inside.

Its brown silken lining was clean, the material though faded retained a hint of rose scented perfume. The interior was worn with age and also possibly frequent use over a long period of time. The handbag contained three separate compartments. After unfastening the zipper in the middle section, to my surprise and delight I discovered a mirror compact. It struck me as odd that the compact hadn't been found by any of the charity shop staff when the handbag had been donated. The lid of the compact was ornately decorated in the 'Art Deco style', portraying a beautiful lady in black and silver enamel work, her head slightly tilted back as if gazing up towards the stars her pose elegant, a serious expression on the lovely features.

When I opened the compact something fluttered to the floor. Excitedly I picked it up and though it was not entirely unexpected, momentarily shivered as the cold crept along the length of my spine.

The face of my dream lady gazed up at me from the photo with those familiar almost opaque pale blue eyes. Her expression was one of imploring for help. I turned the photograph over to look at the back and was rewarded by the sight of a name printed in neat black letters. The name of the frequent invader of my dreams was Grace Farquar.

Now I possessed concrete proof that this lady had indeed existed. Determination to help Grace filled me with a new sense of purpose. I searched the handbag's two remaining compartments but was disappointed by the fact there was nothing to be found in either. I closed the clasp shut, and fastened the buckle. But instead of returning the handbag to the wardrobe I placed it on the hall coat rack.

That night as I dreamed the now all too familiar scenario Grace spoke to me. This time I heard the note of desperation in her voice, in all its quiet urgency.

'I know you will help me Harriet, but please, please hurry!!'

At 6am I leaped out of bed. Instead of heading to the bathroom I ran downstairs and picked up the telephone directory from its place on the hall table. Now that I had discovered her address (there was just one single entry for the name Grace Farquar) I decided to pay a visit to where she had lived. The next task would be to track down the place of her burial and somehow do my best to free her restless spirit. After breakfast I pulled the   carrier bag containing the handbag from the coat stand, put on my coat, grabbed my car keys and left the house.

At 8am I pulled up outside 55 Blessington Street. Stepping from the car, my eyes were immediately drawn to an Estate Agents sign standing in the front garden. I walked to the front door and rang the bell several times. No-one answered the door, the house appeared to be empty. I was just about to give up and leave when a neighbour emerged from the house next door she called out.

'Are you looking for Edward Farquar?'

'No, I have never heard of him. I'm here because of Grace Farquar. Could you please tell me where she is buried?'

The shocked look on her face took me by surprise as she blurted out.

'Buried! What do you mean buried? She isn't dead; at least not yet. Edward her nephew left for the hospital a minute or two before you arrived here. He's about to give permission to switch off life her life support machine. It's a month now since she slipped into a coma following the accident. The poor lady fell headlong down the stairs of her home.'

Was it any wonder Grace had begged me to hurry up and help her. All this time the poor lady was lying down in a hospital bed seemingly dead to the world and yet she had miraculously found a way of contacting me through my dreams. I hastily thanked the neighbour for the information then got back in the car. I drove to the hospital as fast as possible without breaking the speed limit. Within minutes I had parked the car and ran at speed through the hospital entrance nearly tripping up in haste my haste to reach the main reception desk.

Seconds later I was in the lift and on my way to Intensive Care. Ding! The 2nd floor doors opened just seconds later. I ran along the corridor searching for the room where Grace lay, anxiously fearing she was soon to be shut down. At the end of the corridor I stopped abruptly nearly falling, as an invisible barrier stopped me in my tracks. Somehow a waiting presence in the room to my right drew me towards it like a radar signal. I peered in through the glass window only to find the lady of my dreams lying there corpse like. I was relieved to notice there was a slight visible movement, she was still alive thankfully. A very slight but visible fluttering in her chest registered the oxygen pumping into her lungs. The only sounds in the room where those of the life support machine hissing and whirring seeming to murmur the droning words.

'Life – death, life – death, life – death, life - death.'

Chanting out the only two choices, as if selecting the right answer on a game show to win the main prize. Which one will it be? Life or death come on take your pick!

Approaching the bed a giant drum set my heart beat pounding, my throat became constricted. Desperate sobs racked my chest causing the tears to escape from my eyes in pure relief but also despair. What do I do now? I thought. Time is running out fast. I knelt beside the bed and whispered in her ear.

'Grace, it's me Harriet. Can you hear me? Please wake up!'

No response! I called out to her in a much louder voice.

'Grace please wake up!'

I kept up a verbal assault willing her eyes to open. In fact any kind of response would do. Hang on! I thought. The sound of footsteps rapidly approaching along the corridor hastened my actions. Time was running out faster than the speed of light. It was now or never. I took the handbag from the carrier bag and placed it in Grace's hands, then closed her fingers around the handles. A delicate tingling tremor passed through her fingers into mine almost like the sting from brushing against nettles.

In that split second, the door was flung wide open. Suddenly Grace's eyes flickered like the wings of a bird then flew open to reveal the beautiful pale blue eyes. The Doctor, nurse and a dark haired young man took in the scene before them. Each one of their faces registering a look of astonishment. In the case of the young man it was that of horror, his eyes open wide in shock; his body seemed to crumple at the sight before him. He stared at Grace in amazement a silent plea for forgiveness registered clearly on his face. She returned his gaze with a look of accusation!

The scene now became a tableau. No-one moved or spoke as the seconds ticked away. We remained motionless as if frozen in time. Grace broke the spell and the silence. Struggling to speak, her voice a horse whisper, her eyes burned into the young man she croaked out the words.

'Why Edward. Why did you try to kill me?'

Suddenly there was a sense of urgency inside the room, as the scene changed. Understanding dawned quickly, everyone suddenly became aware that Grace's fall down the stairs had not been caused by an accident. Edward tried to break free of the room. But the Doctor moved quickly, he extended his right leg, and tripped up Edward. The Doctor and nurse grabbed his arms and held him on tight. There was no chance of him making an escape. I ran from the room and sped along the corridor dived into an office. I picked up the phone receiver and dialled 999.

After the Police Detective had taken down the statement from Grace, and Edward had been arrested, I returned to her bedside. We searched each other's faces for a long time each willing the other to speak first. Grace was still holding that distinctive cream and brown bag as if her life depended on it and indeed it had been the saviour of hers.

'Grace how did you do it, how did you ever manage to find me?'

She looked at me and smiled there was a twinkle in her eyes.

'My nephew Edward would now be both rich and free if he hadn't been in such a hurry to get rid of all my things. He never could understand my strong attachment to this bag. I first set eyes on it in a strange dream many years ago. The very next day I seen it in a shop window display and felt compelled to buy it. As I held it in my hands that first time, a tingling sensation ran through my fingers and along the length of my arms. Somehow I knew that this handbag would play an important part in my destiny. As to how you and I made contact Harriet, that's a mystery most likely never to be solved, but one for which I will always be grateful!

Haunted House

I lived in dread every single day of the postman arriving on my doorstep. I received no personal mail anymore, no letters, postcards or greetings cards. The only type of mail delivered were brown envelopes containing final demands for bills that remained unpaid. Since Harry left I had soon come to realise the lavish lifestyle we had shared for the previous six months had been funded by a multitude of credit cards. He scarpered a fortnight ago and hasn't been seen or heard from since.

There was no indication that his departure was imminent. A quick peck on the cheek and a friendly smiling 'cheerio' and he was gone. I didn't worry until the early hours, thinking he must have been involved in some sort of accident. There was not a single reply to any of my texts and frantic phone calls. He must be badly injured, there was no other explanation as to why my messages would be totally ignored. As the dawn light streamed in through the bedroom window I decided it was time to contact the police.

It was much later as I passed the utility room and noticed the keys to his S Type Jaguar were still hanging on the key hook: that my suspicions sent alarm bells clanging like the peels of Big Ben. Why would he leave his precious car here, it didn't make sense to me. I raced up the stairs and headed for our bedroom, opened the door of the walk in wardrobe. A sudden realisation hit me. He hadn't had an accident; just deserted and taken the coward's way out by not bothering to say a proper goodbye. The rails of the wardrobe were crammed full of his collection of bespoke suits and silk shirts. The handmade Italian leather shoes were stacked in neat rows on the shelf. The drawers contained expensive underwear and silk socks. It was obvious to me he was not about to return anytime soon though, when I discovered the small leather suitcase was missing. Whatever he had packed had been the bare minimum and done without my noticing a thing. Obviously he had good reason to make a hasty exit!

The S Type had been repossessed the day after he left. The bailiffs had taken the furniture, television, computer and everything else that was not nailed to the ground. I was living in a flat which was almost empty save for the fitted kitchen and bathroom. My bank account was now empty and my job did not pay anywhere near enough to cover the rest of the debts. I leaned on the windowsill with a cup of tea in my hand and wished there was some quick and easy way out of this dilemma. At that precise moment the letter box opened and it was a relief to find there were no brown envelopes being delivered today. A flyer lay on the polished wooden parquet floor.

I picked up the flyer and unfolded it. A monochrome photo of a sinister mansion almost filled the A4 sheet. A headline above the roof read (Le Fleurs Du Mal Manor). Below the picture, a question was written in bold black copperplate gothic script.

'Are you brave enough to spend the night alone in Britain's most haunted house?'

I turned the flyer over to read the details on the back. A major TV Company was offering £5000 to anyone who was willing to spend a full 24 hours, living in the haunted house. Not just any house; but the house which had been the location for numerous sightings and countless apparitions. It had gained the nickname (Spook Central). Various brief accounts of the many terrifying visions were also clearly detailed. There was a phone number printed at the bottom of the page plus an email address.

My computer had gone the way of all the other valuables in the flat, but I did have a few pounds in credit on the mobile. I didn't believe in ghosts, spirits, apparitions or any other sort of paranormal activity. If there was a category in the Guinness Book of Records for the worlds' biggest cynic then my name would appear within its pages under that very title. I quickly phoned the TV Company and a little flutter of sheer joy beat fast wings inside my heart. I was finally going to be able to start afresh and put the past and my debts behind me, that £5000 prize was mine for the taking. I could move away to a new town far from here and put paid to the recent past. I was young enough, only 25 years old, not bad looking with my bright green eyes, pale cream skin and long dark hair. My figure was not perfect but did go in and out in all the right places. I had no relatives, no attachments. My parents had died in a car accident together just three years previously. A tear threatened to slip from my eye and hastily it was wiped away. I would never stop missing them but life had to go on being lived. No time for what ifs? It was time to face reality and build a new life for myself with hopefully a great future.

The three weeks (since the phone call to the TV Company) had passed in a whirlwind of activity. I had paid off as many bills as possible. The flat had been repossessed by the building society and I had moved into the YWCA on a temporary basis with my very few possessions packed in a holdall. The TV Company had sent a limousine for me, it arrived outside the YWCA and I was ready and eager to set off on this new adventure. My case was packed and I walked out into bright morning sunlight. The flash of TV cameras were trained on me and I stood proud with my head held high. Later when the limousine pulled up outside the allegedly Haunted House I stepped from the car and the interviewer came forward with the camera crew. Eddie Parker was a good looking man and a natural for television with that easy confidence he displayed and his friendly manner, which endeared me to him right away.

'Good morning Eve how are you feeling now that it's almost time to enter the house?'

'I have absolutely no apprehensions about spending 24 hours in the house. As far as I am concerned ghosts don't exist.'

'There are many stories of seriously terrifying spirits, in Le Fleurs Du Mal Manor. The previous owner left after six months, vowing to never to set foot inside the place again. Months later he set about writing a book about his experiences that eventually became a best seller. The house has remained empty for the last ten years. No-one has entered the place in all that time but the stories of sightings are still too numerous to be ignored, are you sure you don't want to change your mind?'

'No! Eddie there is no question of me changing my mind. I really need that £5000 and have absolutely no qualms whatsoever!'

A slight cold breeze ran along the length of my spine as the last word was spoken. I had to admit to myself that this was the first time since the phone call to the TV Company; that there was the teeniest doubt in my mind as to the decision I took to go ahead and stay in the house. I glanced up at the dark grey stone facade. The house looked cold and uninviting despite the morning sunlight. The mansard roof of dark slate tiles had four dormer windows. Each window had a circular stained glass window pane depicting flowers with vibrant red petals.

The flowers gave the house its name (Le Fleurs Du Mal) or the Flowers of Evil. I became aware of Eddies' voice saying something but I hadn't quite heard the words. I turned towards him and flashed a somewhat forced smile of confidence.

'I'm ready to go in Eddie see you tomorrow at 8'o clock sharp.'

He smiled and stood next to me for a few moments to pose for the camera crew.

'Who knows what the next 24 hours have in store for Eve Stevens. Le Fleurs Du Mal Manor is without a doubt thee; most haunted house in Britain!

See you tomorrow Eve and best of luck. This is Eddie Parker saying goodbye for now.'

I heard him whisper a quick!

'Let's hope I will see Eve tomorrow!'

The TV crew remained silent as they watched me walk the last few yards down the drive towards the great manor house. As I reached the front door my hand pushed the handle down and it clicked open surprisingly easy. I flashed a smile towards the TV crew then turned and stepped inside. The door slid closed behind me and I gulped in surprise at the sight of the most beautiful entrance hall ever seen. Just ahead was a wonderfully curved, highly polished central mahogany staircase, which led up to the next floor. The wood practically gleamed. I imagined ladies sweeping up and down the wide steps in beautiful ball gowns wearing glittering jewels. At the top of the staircase was another circular window depicting the same flowers in vibrant red petals but they certainly did not look evil. The sun shone through the window bathing the hall in a warm glow and my spirits lifted considerably.

There were many portraits hanging in the hall on the tall wood panelled walls. None of the faces were in any way sinister, with kindly features smiling in serene contentment. I was more than a little confused about this house. I had expected the interior to be dark and sinister, full of cobwebs and dark shadows. An aura of peace and sense of great happiness overwhelmed me. Strangely I was filled with content and felt comfortable in the surroundings. Even though I didn't believe in spirits this house was definitely not what was expected.

As my thoughts drifted along I heard the sound of footsteps close behind me. I could not believe my eyes when on turning around a butler appeared, walking towards me dressed in the smartest uniform. He was tall, of slim build, with dark hair cut into a neat style. His facial features were more aristocratic than any peer of the realm I had ever seen on the television. His clothes were beautifully pressed, his black leather shoes gleamed from ceaseless polishing .I could see my face reflected in the shine. He beamed a smile saying.

'Can I take your case madam and show you to your suite? My name is Cardew.'

I was struck dumb for a moment at the unexpected but no less welcome sight of another human being. What was going on here? The TV Company had obviously manufactured those stories of the most haunted house in Britain. It must be some sort of reality show where the cameras were well hidden but obviously filming everything that happened over the next 24 hour period. They would probably have actors appearing in the early hours of the night trying to frighten the wits outs of me. The proverbial penny quickly dropped. Oh Yes! This was a show alright and I was the star. Well if they thought I was going to forfeit that £5000 prize and run scared from this house they had another think coming. I would play along with their game and tomorrow that £5000 would be mine.

'Thanks Mr Cardew that's very kind of you.'

'You are most welcome Miss Stevens and it's just Cardew!'

I followed him up the sweeping staircase and a steely determination enveloped me in the power of a super hero. No matter what happened I was not about to set foot outside this house until 8 o'clock tomorrow morning. We walked along the left hand side of the corridor until we reached a room with a double door entrance. Cardew put the case down and opened both doors with a theatrical flourish, standing aside to allow me to enter the room first. The sumptuous surroundings brought forth gasps of delight and I skipped like a child around the room taking in the sight of blue silk wallpaper and curtains of oriental damask. The massive bed with the curved headboard was covered in the same damask as the curtains, pleated into a fan shape. The bedding was of equally rich material and luxurious. The room contained a wonderfully stylish suite of furniture and a full length mirror with an ornate gilded antique frame. I noticed an oil painting above the bed. It was a portrait of a lady with features strangely so similar to mine that her resemblance to myself was uncanny.

Cardew stepped into the room and opened another set of double doors leading to an en-suite bathroom. He smiled and nodded as I walked into the most luxurious bathroom imaginable. It was a real delight for me to see that the circular porcelain bath also doubled as a Jacuzzi. I could imagine those powerful water jets pummelling my skin and would be diving in there at the first opportunity. The walk in shower was enormous. The sink and vanity unit were like something from an old Hollywood movie, the golden framed mirror was surrounded by circular lights. The walls were of a sunshine yellow, the curtains of gold silk reached to the floor. The carpet was of a black and gold pattern its pile deep and soft. My smile grew even wider as I took in every small detail of the magnificent room.

'Miss Stevens, breakfast will be served at 9 o'clock in the main dining room. He handed me a sheet of paper. Here is a plan of the house so you don't have any trouble finding your way. There is a bell pull in the bedroom don't hesitate to ring should you need anything else.'

'Thanks Cardew, all this luxury is both overwhelming and wonderful. This is not at all how I imagined it to be!'

Cardew left the room and I pinched myself to make sure this was real and not some marvellous dream. The TV Company had certainly gone to great expense for this show. I fully realised that later there would be something very unpleasant in store for me, otherwise it wouldn't be much of a programme. Viewers of reality TV tuned in for the shock value and enjoyed the spectacle, of its so called stars of the show being set up for humiliation. I was determined to keep my resolve and deal with whatever they had in store for me, with a calm air of dignity. I glanced at my watch surprised to find only fifteen minutes had passed since entering the house. I could not resist a quick dip in the Jacuzzi. This was the one place cameras would not be installed. Surely even TV Companies would not stoop that low.

At 8.55am I was dressed and ready to go downstairs. The pangs of hunger suddenly gnawed at my stomach. I walked along the corridor down the sweeping staircase and made my way to the main entrance hall. A door to the right led to another corridor, at the end of which I noticed a set of very tall double doors with ornate brass handles. I opened the right hand door and stepped into the dining room. The table was large enough to seat at least twenty people. It was adorned with the finest crystal glass and china but with only one place setting at the far end of the table. A large cabinet along the main wall contained an array of silver dishes with lids, I headed straight for them with a plate in my hand. I filled the plate with bacon, eggs, kidneys and mushrooms then took a seat at the table. The door opened and Cardew entered carrying a tray laden with a pot of tea, milk jug, sugar bowl and a rack with freshly toasted bread cut into triangles. I thanked him and he acknowledged it with a slight bow, before heading out the door leaving me to enjoy the delicious breakfast.

I ate the tasty food and drank the hot tea with relish. Even the lavish lifestyle enjoyed for six months with Harry had not extended to this level of luxury. I left the table and decided to take a tour of the surroundings. There must be plenty of rooms in a house this size and I was a naturally curious type of person I took the map from my pocket and headed out of the dining room. Most of the rooms on the ground floor had large French style windows overlooking neat formal gardens. It seemed such a shame to be stuck indoors on such a beautifully sunny day but the thought of my £5000 prize wiped away any disappointment about staying indoors.

I explored the second floor and each and every room was beautifully decorated in the most luxurious style. Whoever owned this house now must be immensely rich. For the first time I wondered why it was that my curiosity had not extended to researching the property, before agreeing to stay here. I knew the answer to that. Desperation for money had been my driving force these past few weeks and that £5000 had blinkered me to everything else.

 I took the staircase to the third and last floor curious to enter the rooms behind the dormer windows. I was eager to see close up their circular stained glass panels of flowers with vibrant red flowers. I opened the door to find a large nursery, the walls were decorated with scenes from fairy tales. There were a couple of small single beds along one wall of the room and an antique baby's cot on rockers. There was an old fashioned wooden rocking horse, a metallic pedal car and a large box filled with toys. Part of the room was divided into a study area complete with desks and chairs. A large blackboard on a stand dominated the area at the end of the room. There wasn't even one speck of dust visible in the room. I found it really bothered me to notice the beds and cot were made up with fresh clean linen, as if awaiting a baby and small children. I shivered for a fleeting moment. Through the windows the sun still shone brightly and the warm glow from the red light of the flower petals swept away my melancholy mood.

The day wore on and I spent the time alone in the house. Cardew and any other staff in the house worked quietly behind the scenes. There was luncheon served in the dining room, followed later by afternoon tea served in the drawing room. I had never eaten so much food in my life, but still found myself eagerly looking forward to dinner later in the day. I yawned loudly, mouth open wide! All this luxurious living was so exhausting! That thought made me giggle. I made my way back to my room and lay down on the bed, and found myself drifting off to sleep almost immediately.

Much later I awoke from the most disturbing dream. Beads of perspiration slid across my brow, to drip down my cheeks and neck, the collar of my blouse felt clingy and damp. The split second my eyes fluttered open, the substance of my dream slipped from memory but the echo of fear lasted seconds longer. I roused myself and was shocked to find shadows lurking all around the room. How could it be dark so soon? This was July, the days were long and the sun did not set until late evening. Surely I could not have slept for so many hours.

Now I understood, it was all to do with timing. I realised the entertainment was about to start. The actors were probably lying in wait ready to play their part and appear before me as ghosts and ghouls determined to drive me out of this house. The TV Company would no doubt have a crew hidden out of sight in the grounds, cameras at the ready to start filming the haunting and my hasty exit when the terror grew too much for this self-confessed sceptic.

I went into the bathroom and took a quick shower, brushed my teeth, blow dried my hair and applied a fresh layer of make-up before the illuminated mirror. I caught a glimpse of shadow behind me and turned to see a woman in long grey dress, blood dripping from the knife embedded in her chest. The woman wailed like a banshee and loomed towards me her face a mask of sheer terror. That's because it is a mask I thought, good grief how corny could you get?

'Look miss, you've done your best, but you may as well give up now. I am going nowhere and you can pass that message on to the rest of the cast of (Hire a Haunting) that £5000 prize is mine.'

It was spooky the way she disappeared in a puff of smoke, very impressive special effects I reluctantly had to admit. I put on my one and only best dress, then made my way out into the corridor once more. Awaiting me was a character wearing a vampire costume complete with long black cloak revealing a red silk lining. Well obviously the message had not been passed on by Miss Grey Dress. As I drew close to him, he opened his mouth to reveal long, sharp, blood stained fangs. I pulled my shoulders up, straightened my back and stared directly into his strangely amber coloured eyes.

'Don't even try to put the frighteners on me, you are wasting your time. I am staying in this house until 8'o clock tomorrow morning, nothing will drive me away.'

He veered towards me; eyes shining with pure malice. His mouth opened wide, fangs exposed to the full. He leaned in towards my neck then suddenly backed off shielding his face. Then strangely he seemed to shrink before my very eyes and transformed into a bat before flying off. That was a bit more like it. A really great piece of acting I thought, while briefly touching the gold crucifix hanging on the chain at my neck.

I walked into the dining room and was surprised to find every place at the table was set. Who else was on the guest list? Of course I guessed right away! It suddenly dawned on me that Cardew the butler, was also a member of the cast! He was a fine actor that was certain, playing his character to perfection. I sat down at the head of the table and one by one the other guests' arrived, each a more terrifying vision than the one previous. The headless cavalier put on a stunning performance. A woman dressed head to toe in black wore a veil which could not obscure a terrifying countenance. Each and every one of the actors put on a show worthy of a BAFTA award. Cardew served the five course meal in a quietly dignified manner and smiled each time I politely thanked him. He studied my face in detail and registered mild surprise at the way I tried to engage the other guests into polite conversation. Later after the last course had been eaten, I bid each of the guests a pleasant 'good night' and headed back to the comfort of my luxurious room. Once inside I found yet more actors awaiting me, one in my bed laid out like a corpse, one in my bath; embarrassingly naked with a noose about his neck. There was a woman slumped in the shower, drenched in blood from the gash which had almost severed her neck. Now I had had just about enough and felt really very angry!

'Enough is enough it has been a long day and I have been very polite but my patience has now come to an end. Will you all please get the hell out of my room and the bathroom and let me have some peace!'

I clapped my hands together loudly and shooed them all away out into the corridor, then slammed the doors behind them. I changed into my pyjamas and slipped between the cool silk sheets. I put my foam ear plugs in place to help drown out the blood curdling screams, the dreadful wailing and the noisy clanging of chains.

I woke once more to a bright summer's day. The sun shone brightly through the windows bathing the room in light and warmth. I was much too tired last night to bother closing the curtains. Hang on though, there were no curtains. There was no furniture in the room either apart from the camp bed I was lying on. I walked into the bathroom to find an old tub with clawed feet, and old fashioned toilet with a wooden seat and overhead cistern. The stained white porcelain sink was meshed with a series of fine cracks, and there was no plug to be seen. I washed, got dressed and packed my bag. The TV Company were absolutely amazing, how did they manage to make all these changes in the few hours I had been asleep? I heard the sound of a bell clanging and loud knocks coming from the front door. I flew down the rickety old staircase with broken banister rails. The entrance hall was dark and dingy; the portraits which hung on the walls were covered in cobwebs. I opened the door somewhat surprised to notice the blanched white face of Eddie Parker.

'Jesus Christ Eve what happened it's 10 o'clock? I have been hammering on the door and ringing the bell intermittently for the past two hours!'

It was then I noticed the police car coming up the drive.

'Eve, how are you feeling this morning, are you okay?'

'I'm just fine and ready to receive my £5000 prize. Those actors you hired certainly worked hard for their money. I hope they were well paid for their services. I was surprised you tried so hard to drive me out. Still it spurred me on to be all the more determined not to fall for the obviously fake haunting. How did you manage to transform the house from luxurious mansion to a derelict ruin overnight? That was absolutely amazing!'

One look at Eddie's bewildered expression explained everything. Le Fleurs Du Mal Manor, was indeed the most haunted house in Britain and there was doubt now of the existence of ghosts and spirits. It was now time to collect the prize money and get far away from here and as quickly as possible.

She was just about to throw the flier into the bin, when Sadie noticed the leaflet wasn't an item of the usual junk mail received on an almost daily basis. The leaflet contained details of an Art Exhibition that was due to take place in the local park. She was relieved to find that the Exhibition would not be exposed to the open air. Every item of artwork would be displayed undercover inside a large marquee. Considering the hot sunshine and unusually high temperatures at the moment she didn't relish the thought of becoming sunburnt. Her skin tone was naturally very pale. It required very brief exposure to the strong sunlight for her pale cream skin to turn to a shade of boiled lobster. The entrance fee was just £3 and there would be at least sixty paintings on display. She had gradually developed a great interest in art since becoming a student at the local college. It would be useful to suss out the competition and gauge an idea of how much her own pictures might be worth.

The following Saturday at 10 o'clock on a bright and sunny July day, she joined the long queue lined up waiting to buy tickets for the exhibition. She was both surprised and pleased to discover so many people taking an interest in the works of art. The queue rapidly dwindled and a few minutes later she handed over her £3 entry fee in exchange for a ticket. The refreshment area in the marquee was largely empty, so she decided it would be a good idea to sit down for a while and enjoy a cup of coffee. A brochure had been placed on each table which enabled the visitor to view photos of the pictures in the exhibition before viewing the originals.

She added a spoonful of sugar to the coffee cup and stirred it clockwise with her right hand, while turning quickly to the first page of the brochure with her left. The glossy introduction page of the brochure showed a marvellous painting of a seascape featuring an old fashioned wooden galleon at the centre.

Tidal waves hammered the massive wooden hull that veered dangerously to the side nearly upending it. The waves rose up high into the sky before crashing downwards and almost engulfed the ship in its powerful white surf. She imagined how it must be for the sailors living and working on the ships during those terrible storms. They had no way of knowing if they would survive the journeys to foreign lands thousands of miles away. The voyages that took months, sometimes years at a time.

Her thoughts wandered, she imagined an old ship its captain at the helm barking orders while the poor crew worked like slaves to carry them out. A scene unfurled in her mind of a sailor climbing up the rigging to the crows' nest; clinging on tightly to the ropes while battling high winds and driving rain, until the safety of the perch was reached. Then with hands cupped shielding his eyes from the rain he peered far out to sea hoping to see a land mass not too far away. The wind lashing the wooden hull of the ship until it almost capsized. The dramatic scene unfolded, bolts of lightning and driving rain lashed down on the heads of those poor souls below. It seemed so real for a moment, she could almost hear the voices of those men as they struggled to keep the ship afloat and sailing sure on the plotted course. In those far off days, travelling the vast oceans and seas of the world was such a dangerous death defying feat. Those vast ships at the mercy of the tides and elements ventured out to circumnavigate the world, unknowing of the dangers they could be forced to endure. She silently acknowledged the bravery of those sailors in bygone days who travelled the globe fraught with so much danger, transporting all that precious cargo from far off lands.

Her thoughts wandered for a few moments then returned to the seascape painting. She peered closely and savoured every tiny detail. Sadie had great respect for the artist who had perfectly captured the drama of the scene.

Page two of the brochure presented a landscape painting. A picture of far off hills, green pastures, cattle and sheep grazing. The summer sun bathing the scene in its warmth and light. A large pond in the foreground caught my gaze, its surface shimmering with glints of sunlight dancing on the dark blue water like tiny stars twinkling. That painting conjured up all the peace and tranquillity of the countryside in an idyllic rural setting. Just gazing at the picture lulled her into a state of calm relaxation.

She turned the page to discover the next painting was an abstract canvas. It was a hodgepodge of bright colour shapes and splodges of paint, seemingly thrown at the canvas with no sense of order or perspective. This picture conjured up pure chaos, which jangled at the nerve endings and she found nothing to admire within it.

Once more she turned the page. The following painting depicted a scene of the seaside, the setting of which was in the modern day. A mother and child sat on the golden sandy beach both wearing similar cotton summer dresses of white with blue polka dots. The child was touching her mother's arm with one hand trying to draw attention to the sand castle she had built and was so proud of. The child's mother held on tightly to a mobile phone. The hand held device had her full attention, as her fingers were poised over the keypad ready to send a text or make a call. She was totally oblivious to the young child whose little face registered such sad disappointment. The title of this painting was so appropriate, it was named (Indifference). Though it was just a picture sadly there was an element of reality about the scene. She closed the pages of the brochure and laid it on the table for the next visitor.

The coffee cup was now drained and Sadie pushed the cup and saucer aside as she pushed her chair back and stood up. She was eager to see all the paintings on display and made her way through to the exhibition area. Despite the fact that there was quite a large crowd, most people stared briefly at each picture in turn then moved quickly on to the next so there was hardly any waiting involved. Sadie studied each of the paintings in depth and picked up a few tips regarding brush technique and composition. She had no intention of copying any artists' work but it was interesting to note the varying styles. She also made a mental note of the monetary value of each picture, considering the time frame it may have taken to complete.

Approaching the last half dozen of the exhibits, Sadie felt a sudden and inexplicable urge to forego viewing the remaining paintings. She headed straight to the last one on display which was perched on an antique wooden easel. It was a painting in oils and depicted a grand mansion. Vast formal gardens could be seen in the foreground, while the mansion itself was bordered by trees in uniform rows neatly spaced.

Her eyes were drawn to the signature of the artist at the bottom right hand corner of the painting, she gasped in utter surprise. The artists name in fine black italic script that was coincidentally the same as her own style of handwriting. The full inscription read. An image of Blessington Hall 1914, painted by Sadie Simmons. Exactly 100 years previously a woman bearing her name had studied art and painted this magnificent picture. The twist of fate was nothing short of amazing! A century separated the pair, yet they were both artists bearing the same name. Such a similarity had to be more than just mere coincidence. She shivered momentarily feeling unexpectedly chilled as if a ghost had brushed past her and come to close.

Sadie could almost hear the mechanisms of her brain busily ticking like clockwork   in a frenzy of activity. The neutrons of the brain set in motion illuminated by curiosity, darting at great speed like the ball- bearings in a pinball machine. How could it be possible that she was standing here in 2014 staring at a painting bearing her own signature? Realisation dawned with the clarity of a halogen bulb that the hand writing exactly matched that of her own.

Sadie had always been proud of her handwriting and received many compliments on the flourishing calligraphy. The curled lettering flowed across the corner of the painting in exactly the same style, the (I's) were dotted and the (T's) crossed in the precise position as her own.

Sadie peered more closely at the oil painting. She noticed a subtle change taking place on the canvas as her gaze became more intense. There was something intriguing about the house which caught her full attention. What was it? She scrutinised the building in more detail noticing every centimetre of it. She started to examine the picture thoroughly beginning with the entrance on the ground floor, peering meticulously at each window on that level. The second floor was also inspected thoroughly, every minute detail carefully inspected. Sadie was astonished at the magnificent fine art work and attention to detail in every single window frame. Each window was in correct perspective set among the red bricks of this magnificent mansion. It was just at the moment when she raised her eyes to the attic windows that there seemed to be movement behind an arch shaped window pane of stained glass. The window was set in the very centre of the house. A closer look showed a tiny figure stood before an easel, a paint brush hovering in mid- air towards the picture set on the stand.

She was mesmerised by the tiny figure and moved even closer, her nose almost touched the large canvas before her. Sadie tripped over the stand of the easel and somehow must have blacked out momentarily. On opening her eyes it was a shock to find that she was no longer in the marquee, but lying on the floor of an unfamiliar vaulted ceilinged room. She rubbed her eyes and pinched the flesh on the back of her hand but this was no dream. Where was this place? How had she got there? How could she get back?

The girl standing above her was just as shocked to find Sadie suddenly appearing in her room. Both Sadie and the girl were also astonished to discover they could be identical twins. They shared the same wavy blonde hair, both had eyes the exact shade of hazel, they shared identical features, their height and figures were just as equal, their likeness to each other was uncanny! The only difference between them was their style of clothing. Sadie was dressed in 21st century clothing. The other girl wore an outfit better suited to the distant past. Sadie picked herself up from the floor and shook off the dust from her clothing. Both girls found their voices at that moment. Sadie allowed the other girl to speak first. The girl (who seemed to be from the past) spoke in the cultured accent of an aristocrat.

'To say I am shocked by your sudden appearance is an understatement. Yet strangely it seems to me that maybe somehow you were expected to be here, though for what purpose I cannot imagine. I could not rid myself of the inkling that something special was about to happen this very day. Are you by any chance an artist?'

'I'm a second year art student at the local college. I have no idea as to how I managed to be transported to this place, but it seems that I've been roped into a scene from some kind of historical television drama judging by your style of dress. How could it be possible that I've simply and inexplicably fallen directly into this room? Just seconds ago I was staring through the painted windows of a picture at the art exhibition. I was astonished to see a tiny figure poised before a canvas holding a paintbrush. I leaned forward and narrowed my eyes for a closer look. The next instant my eyes opened wide to find you standing above me just as deeply shocked by my unexpected arrival as I am.'

'I certainly cannot answer the question of how you arrived here, but now that you are I would appreciate your advice on something. Please do take a look at this painting. Your arrival could not be more fortuitous. I am experiencing some difficulty moving on to the next stage of this particular picture.'

Sadie turned her gaze towards the painting. It came as no surprise to find it was the picture which drew all her attention at the exhibition. There was an obvious difference though between the one in the marquee and the one standing on the easel. This painting had the spaces marked out for the location of where the windows would be placed. The only difference being as yet there was no actual detail inside the window spaces.

'This is the exact same painting that was on display at the exhibition. This is the painting that drew all my attention before I tripped over the easel it was displayed on. This place has to be (Blessington Hall). You just have to be Sadie Simmons the artist. Bizarrely we both share the same name as well as identical looks. The thing is Sadie, I was at the exhibition just seconds ago and the date today is July 7th 2014. Judging by your style of dress I presume it's not the year 2014 in this place?' The other girl was equally astonished!

'Sadie there is no rational explanation whatsoever as to how you could have arrived here but I can assure you that the date today is definitely July 7th 1914!'

The two girls soon began to speak animatedly and at length until a knock at the door brought the conversation to an abrupt end. Sadie pointed to a large cabinet and the girl from the future stepped inside it and closed the door. A parlour maid entered the room carrying a tray laden with a tea set, a cake stand and a plate of finely cut sandwiches. She set down the tray on a short legged table close to the arched window of the attic studio.

'Oh I beg your pardon miss! I only brought one cup not knowing you have company.'

'There is no-one else here Molly I am quite alone.'

'I thought I heard you talking to someone else miss. My mistake enjoy your tea.'

The very second the door closed behind the maid Sadie stepped from the cabinet. The two young women smiled and giggled in a conspiratorial friendly manner.

Sadie mentioned it had been a while since she had drunk a cup of coffee. She gratefully accepted a cup of tea but declined the offer of a sandwich. She was much too excited by the events of the present to feel any pangs of hunger. They chatted easily and animatedly for a while, exchanging the basic facts about each other. Some while later both girls turned their gazes towards Sadie's unfinished painting. She explained that her expertise did not extend to the fine detailed brushwork needed to paint the mullioned windows, nor the interior scene beyond the panes of glass.

Her companion immediately offered to help. Hoping that Sadie (1914) was willing to trust her to paint the canvas. The artist handed her an old fashioned painting smock of the kind she had only ever seen in pictures, or old book illustrations. The voluminous white smock with the large black pussy cat bow at the neck was cumbersome, but she removed the belt from her jeans nipping the material at her waist and rolling the vast sleeves into neat cuffs above the elbows. She set to work right away mixing the appropriate shades needed for authenticity. Taking the finest narrow paint brush she started to draw the scene which would appear through the first window on the ground floor. Before long she had moved onto the second window and then progressed to the third.

The attic room was now beginning to look quite murky as the afternoon light faded. The evening begun to draw shadows along the walls and the ceiling above. Sadie lit the oil lamps and placed them about the room adding much needed light to illuminate the gloom of sundown. She studied the painting and smiled with sheer delight, at the progress her namesake had already accomplished.

The striking of the grandfather clock sounded from the hall. Its chimes shocked her into realising it was already 6 o'clock. Sadie's impromptu arrival had occurred hours ago. The girl must be both weary and very hungry by now.

She had better return to her room and change into another outfit more suitable to wear for dinner. The family members would become suspicious if she did not arrive in the dining hall by 7 o'clock, on the dot. One way or another she would arrange to smuggle some food and a drink up to the attic room. She would also have to supply a pillow and some blankets. There was a very comfortable chaise long which would be an ideal place for the other Sadie to sleep on.

What if the other Sadie had already decided to find a way back to her own time, what then? That very thought prompted a wave of unaccustomed sadness to wash over her. Already the pair had formed a genuine bond in their brief space of time together, but it was unthinkable that they could remain together for long. Even in a house of this size it would be nigh on impossible to keep this great secret for any length of time. A complete stranger from the future suddenly arriving for an impromptu visit, this was a pretty enormous secret. If the other Sadie happened to be seen, how could either of them give a reasonable explanation as to the fact that both girls were mirror images of each other? An even more preposterous idea was the inescapable fact that the other Sadie had somehow managed to travel through time, precisely 100 years into the future!

The days slipped by all too quickly and both girls revelled in the company of one another. They took great delight in the shared secret of living in close proximity under the same roof. It was remarkable that their precious days carried on in joyful companionship, under the very noses of a household filled with many members of family and staff. Yet there was no hint that anyone suspected the presence of an unexpected guest in the house.

The painting of Blessington Hall had quickly become a joint venture. Just two weeks later it was finally completed. The girls stepped back from the canvas. Each window pane and scene within was highlighted in detail. The brickwork and every other aspect of the house was completely and authentically replicated in oils. Both girls experienced a range of emotions as they stood side by side admiring the picture depicting the great mansion in all its glory. They both experienced immense pride in their joint efforts to paint such a fine piece of art. It was a cause of great sadness for them both, knowing they would soon be parted. There was also a feeling of gratitude for the great friendship they had relished. The girls embraced each other with warm affection, the emotion somehow now more poignant. Instinctively they both realised this contact would be their last.

When at last the embrace came to an end, Sadie was unsurprised to find herself standing alone in the attic studio. The present day Sadie found herself once more in the exhibition marquee staring at the painting of (Blessington Hall). She was filled with pride in the beautifully painted windows, but more than a little sad at the loss of such a wonderful friendship. A brief glance at her watch revealed that no time at all had passed in this century since she had been away. This was astonishing considering the fact she had enjoyed a whole fortnight living in the summer of 1914.

As she glanced at the arched window of the attic something stirred behind the glass pane. She thought it must be her imagination running wild. Maybe it was just a trick of the light. But it was neither of those things. An almost invisible hand flipped the catch on the attic window then opened it slightly. The hand pushed an envelope through the gap which then fluttered to the ground. As Sadie glanced to the floor a white envelope landed right at her feet. The letter written in the distinctive script so familiar to her, was addressed to Miss Sadie Simmons. With trembling fingers she tore open the envelope. It seemed so strange to be reading a letter that her friend had written a century ago, considering the black ink from the pen she had used was barely dry!

Blessington Hall,

Buckinghamshire.

July 7th

Dear Sadie,

The painting of Blessington Hall belongs to you. Even though we were together such a short time I made the decision to bequeath it to you in my will. I have no idea if you are my reincarnated soul or hopefully a future descendant of mine, who knows? But you deserve to receive this legacy. After all it was a joint effort. I will never forget these past two weeks we have spent together, even if I live to be a hundred years old.

If you wish to sell the painting then you have my blessing. I would like to think that you will keep it just for a short while in honour of the time we spent together. Take care of yourself my good friend. One day I am sure you will become a famous artist.

Yours very sincerely

Sadie Simmons

X

P.S. I could not help but smile at the incongruity of writing a letter to Sadie Simmons, from Sadie Simmons. Already you are sorely missed.

Sadie put the letter back into the envelope and went to speak to an official. The painting was soon withdrawn from the sale. It belonged to her now and she would never part with it.

Let Me Out!

George was alarmed to find himself lying down on a mattress in the unlit room.
He was confined to this space by the wooden bars surrounding him on all four
sides. Completely helpless he was unaware of how much time had passed, since
this dire situation had become apparent. There was no pillow on the mattress
just a sheet underneath him, a light blanket was draped over his body. His head
felt like a lead weight, far too heavy to raise up from the mattress. He tried to
manoeuvre his body to face the opposite side, but the effort proved too much of
a strain.

He could not properly distinguish his surroundings, even though his eyes
were now slowly becoming accustomed to the darkness. For some unknown
reason he found himself unable to move his body. It took a supreme effort of
will just to turn his head from one side to the other. He stared up at the ceiling
and could just about make out a dark shape at the centre. For some strange
reason the object hanging directly above him was unidentifiable. His eyelids
drooped, too weighty to stay open. He was fighting an increasing battle with the
onset of sleep in order to remain awake. The battle was a short one, soon
defeated his eyes closed and he was plunged into oblivion.

Sounds drifted through the chambers of unconsciousness. They were
becoming increasingly more intrusive, invading the realms of his comfortingly
enjoyable dreams. His dark lashes fluttered, or at least tried to. His eyelids
remained closed, stuck fast were the moisture had seeped during sleep. He was
unable to open his eyes fully. He cried out in frustration at the sheer
helplessness of his situation. There was nothing he could do, his energy drained
away far too quickly. The exertion of trying to move his body became too much
of an effort, darkness descended yet again as he once more drifted into sleep.

The man and woman sat at opposite sides of the large wooden table facing each other.

'Don't you think it's about time he said something Steve?'

'I was pretty sure that by now he would have said something, anything! I know it's frustrating but we must try and be patient for the moment! Sooner or later he will break his silence, I am certain of that. Whatever happens we just have to make him talk!'

A sharp click similar in sound to the safety catch being released on a handgun, alerted George from the shelter of his dreams and jolted him back into reality. He strived to turn his weary head in the direction of the door as a chink of light poured into the room. The shadow of a powerfully built tall man, stood in the open doorway filling that space. George realised with certainty his situation was about to change. He was more than a little curious about what would happen next. The tall man released a mechanism and the bars on one side of him slid away. He was conscious of feeling exposed and vulnerable, apprehensive even, of the change in his situation. The man leaned in and picked him up in his powerful arms. Just at that moment   George found he was unable to keep his eyes any open any longer and drifted once more into the total oblivion of unconsciousness.

He became aware of the change of location even before his eyes managed to open and take notice of the surroundings. The intense light, much too bright was almost blinding as it pierced his eyelids and the glare was extremely distressing to say the least. He was aware of the warmth from a moist cloth used to clear the sticky sleep from his eyes. The lashes now free fluttered like the dark wings of a raven, his eyes opened and the scene became all too clear.

To his amazement and utter despair he found himself strapped to a chair, confined by leather straps rendering him even more immobile. The powerfully built man sat opposite staring into his eyes with a look of dogged determination.

Before George had time to contemplate what would happen next, he was soon left in no doubt. The interrogation began in earnest intensity almost immediately. The tall man repeated a barrage of words. It was parallel to a verbal firing squad, guaranteed to wear down any resistance George could muster. The onslaught was relentless. George felt the weariness beginning to descend but the man was determined not to let him drift off into the comforting arms of sleep.

'Sooner or later you will say something George. Of that I am in no doubt. No matter how many attempts you make to resist, there is no way I'm going to allow you to stay quiet for much longer!'

George weakened by the lack of sleep, almost gave in to the powerful looking man's demands that he should start talking. He had just about had enough, and didn't think he could take anymore. He longed for sleep to release him from this impossible situation. His lips parted slightly and the powerful interrogator leaned in a little closer, impatiently waiting to hear what George would say. Disappointingly he found that he was unable to utter a word. His tongue felt much too big for his mouth, he was terribly thirsty and badly in need of a drink. The man stood turned and walked away, leaving George restrained and more uncomfortable than he could possibly imagine. Once again his head became much too heavy for him to support, his chin soon drooped down towards his chest. The dark lashes fluttered first rapidly, then slowed down and eventually became still settling on his cheeks, blocking out the intense glaring light as sleep descended.

He awoke to find the leather straps still restrained him to the chair. A woman sat before him at the table, the bottle twirling teasingly in her hands.

'You must be thirsty by now George I'm sure you would like a drink!'

She waived the bottle before his eyes and his tongue pushed forth from his lips indicating the level of his thirst. His hands twitched nervously. He was desperate to grab the bottle from her hands but she was too far from his reach. He could not bear this much longer. She taunted him, the bottle so close but just not close enough.

'Come on George you only have to say the word and you can have as much to drink as you like!'

He glared at her in sheer defiance more determined than ever not to say a word. She could see it was a waste of time and pushed the bottle towards George's lips and tilted it so the liquid poured too quickly down his dry throat, it seemed as if he would choke. He tried to push the bottle away but the weakness in his arms made his protest ineffectual.

Once more his eyes opened. To his great relief he found himself lying on the mattress in the darkened room. He may be surrounded by a wooden cage but at least it was peaceful. He thought of the man and woman interrogators, they would not give up, he knew that much. He opened his mouth wide and tried in vain to say something, his tongue was still swollen despite the drink poured down his throat by that woman. With a supreme effort he endeavoured to take control of his tongue. After several attempts, just one word emitted from his lips surprising even himself with the unfamiliar sound.

The electronic monitor picked up that one word. The man and woman listened intently then squealed in delight as their baby son George called out 'dada' for the very first time.

Dan woke up long before the alarm clock was due to start beeping and signal the beginning of a new day. He hadn't slept very well to say the least, but it wasn't unexpected, this was due to anticipation rather than trepidation. He genuinely looked forward; with great enthusiasm, to starting his first day of employment as a (Double Glazing) Salesman. As an occupation it had to be admitted, it didn't feature anywhere near the top of the list of his favourite forms of employment. But it was a big step up from the depressing and demeaning status of being unemployed. There was more than a grain of truth in the saying, beggars can't be choosers. A job, any job was preferable to being out of work.

Considering the shortage of vacancies around at the moment, he was just grateful to have found work at long last. Having signed off the Jobseekers Benefit, as soon as his signature was written on the official form; his self-esteem had been restored. A sense of worthiness was just one of those important things in life that money cannot buy. Earning a living and being able to pay his own way was something he could only dream of, with every job application sent out, every C.V. posted, every newspaper advert in the Situations Vacant column applied for! Now at last his perseverance had finally paid off.

At 45, he counted himself lucky to still have a full head of thick sandy hair. With his slightly ruddy complexion from his love of the outdoors, dark brown eyes, slender build and standing 6ft 2inches tall, he cut an imposing figure. He could easily have passed for ten years younger. He had been entirely alone in the world for the past five years, since the premature death of his beloved wife. Neither he nor his wife had any relatives. Both sets of their parents had just the one child each late in life and they had all died within a few years of each other. Dan and his wife in the early days of marriage, had fervently hoped that one day they would have children of their own. Sadly fate had not been kind to them and their hopes had been crushed when they learned this was not to be. He hadn't felt the need or desire to seek out female company as yet, the grief of his loss, even after this length of time was still too painful. To his way of thinking there was no other woman on earth who could hold a candle to his beloved Marie.

They had been true soulmates, each had fallen under the other's spell on their first sight across a crowded dance floor. Dan had been stunned by the beauty of the dark haired girl with piercing green eyes. He felt as if she were somehow a witch, one glance and he was under her spell. Marie was taken aback also by the strength of her feelings when she turned her gaze on Dan. A powerful and unexplained bolt of pure energy burst inside her heart and she was smitten. They almost ran towards each other in their indecent haste to get acquainted. It was a true meeting of two soulmates, they had so many things in common, but also as many differences of opinion, likes, dislikes, and dreams which differed immensely. But the one thing they did have in common was an instant and potent attraction to each other, which rapidly and oh so easily turned from pure desire to a passionate and all consuming love.

Just a few short weeks after their first meeting they married in a Register Office with just a handful of close friends as witnesses and guests. The ceremony was followed by lunch in a pub. The evening was spent dancing in the same night club where they had been lucky enough to have found each other just a short time ago.

Dan decided it was time to put a stop on reminiscences from the past! Today was not about contemplating the memories of events now long gone. This was to be the first day of his future and time for pushing ahead with renewed enthusiasm for living. It was high time to let go of the dreams which can never have any hope of coming to fruition. Today was his fresh start, no more time to waste dwelling on what might have been. Today was the start of a new chapter, in the life of a recently employed Double Glazing salesmen. The latter thought brought a smile to his lips, he never imagined for one second that he would ever be a salesman, let alone one trying to sell Double Glazing! Still despite the product he would do his best to make a success of the job.

Helen picked up the envelope which had only at that precise moment, dropped through the letterbox to land on the highly polished tiles of the hall floor. She carried it into the living room. Then settled in an armchair before slipping a silver letter opener neatly under the edge and slicing through the envelope with great care. The brown envelope contained a letter of apology for the delayed payment, plus a cheque for the full amount from the Insurance Company.

She stared at the cheque now held in her hands and wondered not for the first time what was to become of her life now? What kind of a future could she expect now that she was alone? How was she going to manage the rest of her life?

Eddie her late husband had died just eight weeks previously. The loss of a husband is such a traumatic and totally life changing event. But in her case the loss was not just that of physical presence, the psychological consequences to her daily life were immense. Despite the bill for his funeral being as yet still outstanding; she was not too concerned. It would be settled without further delay, now that the Insurance Company had sent her the cheque! Money or the lack of it was thankfully not of the greatest concern. This house was far too large for one person and she had already decided to sell it and move elsewhere.

Helen and Eddies daughter Jane, was consumed with grief over the death of her beloved father. The complete opposite was true in Helens' case, she was overwhelmed by the emotions of blessed relief now that he was finally out of her life permanently. She wondered why she experienced no guilt for the contentment which had settled on her shoulders like a warm blanket, but she finally realised that all these years of marriage had been more like a prison sentence. So many years wasted doing everything just the way Eddie demanded. Now she relished the independence that widowhood afforded her.

Her love for Eddie had long since diminished, he himself had been the culprit responsible for that. No-one had the slightest inkling that for years he had deliberately and most cruelly tortured her in a mental capacity. He had relished chipping away her confidence bit by bit and crushing her spirit until there was nothing left. No-one who knew him would ever have suspected he was the kind of man capable of such malice, least of all his own daughter!

Jane never tired of reminding Helen how lucky she was to have such a wonderful husband. She dreamed of one day meeting a man with similar attributes to those of her father, her idea of the ideal man to spend her life with. Jane had a brilliant career in Finance, having worked diligently to climb the ladder of success and was now reaping the rewards. At present she immersed herself even further into work as a way of coping with the heartache of bereavement. Yesterday she had flown from London to Berlin for several business meetings which would take place over a fortnight with the directors of a prominent German Bank.

Helen loved her daughter beyond question despite breathing a hefty sigh of relief when they had said their goodbyes. It wasn't easy trying to play the part of grieving widow, which wasn't the case in her experience. Yet for Jane's sake and that of seeming to be lost she thought it justified to at least pretend the death of her husband was cause for sadness. Momentarily she paused for a moment to glance in the ornate mirror hanging above the fireplace in the living room. Her reflection presented an extremely attractive woman. Helen's glossy bobbed hairstyle complimented her light blonde hair. Her figure was slim and toned. The large emerald green eyes and skin complexion were practically flawless.

Her natural bubbly personality had long since been subdued by her manipulative husband. She stared intensely at the face in the mirror but seemingly didn't recognise herself anymore. Who was this strange woman whose reflection she was so familiar with? This unknown woman with her looks, yet no independent thoughts to speak of, a mere shell of her former self before marriage to Eddie had totally transformed her.

Her husband had controlled every single aspect of her life with his once understated, rapidly escalated dominant personality. From the clothes she wore to the brand of make-up used, even her hairstyle! Eddie directed every aspect of her appearance to his exacting standards.

Once upon a time he had appeared to be so wonderful, with his movie idol looks and a personality oozing charm and good manners. The tall dark and handsome of romantic fiction personified. She had fallen for Eddie rapidly, blind to all reason. Literally dazzled by everything about him. She had strolled down the aisle with a heart filled to the brim with love, and a baby bump partially concealed by an overly large bouquet. The honeymoon lasted all of twenty four hours. Eddie's personality chameleon like, changed to reveal his true self almost as soon as the wedding ring was slipped on to her willing finger. Sadly too late she understood, the attraction and eventual imprisonment of a helpless fly when caught in the spiders' web, or the moth to a bright flame.

The doorbell rang jolting her thoughts back to the present. Helen took a last look in the mirror and glimpsed just for a second a glimmer of the woman she had once been. A spark appeared in her emerald green eyes and with it a long lost memory of what it had been like to be herself. She stood to her full height and an unfamiliar and involuntary lifting to her lips formed a smile full of warmth. Helen walked into the hall and with a flourish opened the front door.

Dan waited nervously until the door was opened by the most beautiful woman he had ever set eyes on. He beamed a smile of such warmth it would have thawed the coldest of hearts. Helen was surprised to find a salesman on the doorstep and had never bought anything in her life without first consulting Eddie. Yet his smile had disarmed her momentarily. She had been caught off guard by the stranger on her doorstep with his genuine and sincere smile. There was something about him that was warm and trustworthy. A tiny spark of recklessness soon ignited into a bright flame.

She noticed the handful of (Double Glazing) leaflets clutched tightly in his hand. A rare impulse caused her to act irresponsibly for the first time in twenty five years. Wondrously she experienced a feeling of pure joy and of being carefree!

'Why don't I put the kettle on and you can show me your brochures. One or two of the windows are in need of replacing. My name is Helen, please do come in.'

'Thanks Helen, so far it's been a terrible day but thanks to you it's improved massively. My name is Dan, it's a real pleasure to meet you.'

As he stepped over the threshold they both felt the spark, something similar to a surge of power passed between them like a bright flame. They sensed the same instantaneous thunderbolt of attraction. Helen and Dan's thoughts and feelings were identical. First it was. What just happened? Then. This feels like it was meant to be! They were both eager for a new start!

Jenny and her mum Tina were still taken aback by the knowledge that they had been invited to appear as contestants on 'The Generation Game'. When the letter arrived from the TV studios they seriously thought it was a wind up! Until Tina had rung the number printed on the letter to confirm that they would be happy to appear on the show, she hadn't believed for a moment it was actually genuine. The pair of them were awestruck at the thought they would soon be meeting Bruce Forsythe.

The day finally dawned and Tina and Jenny could hardly believe that this Saturday night they would be appearing on the show, not sitting at home watching it. They had been greeted by a studio assistant and taken to a very comfortable sitting room for tea and sandwiches, while being given a brief outline of what to expect during the programme.

At long last they were escorted to the wings and Bruce announced them as they walked on to the stage and straight into the glare of the spotlights. As they were introduced to him nerves took a hold of them both, they were visibly shaken for a moment or two. Being the consummate professional after a lifetime spent in show business, it took no time at all for Bruce to put them and the other contestants at their ease.

The show was great fun right from the beginning. They soon forgot the cameras, lights, and an audience filled with people as they were caught up in the excitement of the show. They gazed awestruck now as the professional confectioner placed a delicious looking fruitcake on a stand ready to demonstrate how to ice it to perfection. First the marzipan was rolled out cut to fit and spread with a thin layer of jam, then placed carefully on top of the fruit cake and pressed down lightly. Next the firm icing was rolled, shaped, and cut to fit the sides and the round lid placed over the marzipan. Finally a piping bag was filled and the confectioner piped tiny rosettes and curlicues all around the cake, finishing off with an expert flourish as the stand was rotated for the audience to observe.

A round of applause filled the studio and the confectioner beamed a grateful smile in appreciation of the acknowledgment of his unique skill. The icing of the cake had been completed in three minutes flat. Bruce shook the confectioners hand and asked him to remain on set in order to later judge the contestants efforts at icing their own individual fruit cakes. The contestants were given aprons and hats for hygienic reasons.

The contestants were allotted five minutes to complete the task. Within seconds the audience was in hysterics as six contestants tried and failed in spectacular fashion to apply the marzipan to their fruitcakes. There were red faces all around and a set of furrowed brows from the sheer effort of concentration. All the while the big clock ticked away loudly, as each one of them became covered in icing sugar, jam, and wayward bits of marzipan; during the process of completing the task in hand. After the shortest five minutes ever known the buzzer sounded and the contestants stepped away from their tables.

Howls of laughter still filled the studio as the audience observed the sorry looking specimens of patched up icing and piped rosettes that looked nothing like they were supposed to. The contestants though a little embarrassed were just relieved the task was now at an end.

The confectioner judged their efforts with a look of amazement and just a hint of compassion. He was encouraging in his remarks but the low scores revealed just how difficult the contestants had found this particular challenge. Another round of applause from the audience, a few words of thanks from Bruce and the confectioner left the stage along with the contestants. They were allotted a couple of minutes to clean off the icing, jam and marzipan.

The contestants returned to the stage dressed in the appropriate outfits needed for their next challenge to be accomplished. A troop of Morris dancers filed on to the stage wearing elaborate flower bordered hats. Multi coloured streamers hung from their jackets and silver bells were attached to their brightly coloured, beribboned trouser cuffs. They each played the tambourine while dancing energetically to an old English country tune. As the routine came to an end the audience applauded once more with greater enthusiasm.

The dance troop went through their paces in a simplistic routine and then it was time for the contestants to join in. In this task some of the contestants performed much better than the others, having mastered the steps with ease making a pretty good effort to keep up with the professionals. Jenny who had been born unfortunately with two left feet and all the co-ordination of a wooden doll, kept tripping up. She soon lagged behind when the other dancers were centre stage. Jenny managed always to turn left when the other dancers turned right, twirling in the wrong direction and generally making a right pigs' earhole of the routine. The audience were almost in stitches with laughter. Several times Bruce stepped in to help steer her in the right direction but Jenny was lost in a world of her own.

Once more the buzzer sounded and to Jenny's great relief the ordeal had finally come to an end thankfully. It had been the longest five minutes of her life up to this point in time. It came as no surprise when the leader of the dance troupe awarded her just one point for her efforts. But she was so happy to get that particular task out of the way she smiled broadly.   Tina was convinced that she and Jenny had no chance of winning the game. Neither of them were destined to end up in the hot seat watching the conveyor belt roll past loaded with a selection of luxury items which would be very welcome indeed. Still, she thought we have had a wonderful day to remember and someone had to be the loser.

Remarkably the next challenge proved to be the one at which both mum and daughter excelled. The jolly looking butcher demonstrated the technique of making links of pork sausages. The members of the audience were highly amused by this task and most of the laughter was of a distinctly risqué nature, i.e. downright indecent.

As the sausage skins were stuffed Bruce made some hilarious facial expressions which caused ever louder giggles to spread throughout the studio. A cameraman panned out the lens to zoom in on some of the laughing faces of members of the audience. It was plain to see they were loving every minute of the sausage making process.

After just three minutes several links of perfectly uniform sized sausage links were piled up on a metal tray and the applause was such that it rose to the rafters. The butcher (knowing how much innuendo was attached to the noble art of sausage making) looked at the audience members with a highly amused smile planted on his face which stretched from one ear to the other. Bruce Forsythe almost bent double in fits of laughter himself, settled down with difficulty, stemming the giggles and shook the butchers hand with a firm grip.

'Thank you so much for the demonstration that was wonderful. The audience seemed to enjoy it immensely. Will you please stay and judge the contestants?'

'Of course I will. Thanks for inviting me on the show Bruce it's been a real pleasure.'

He walked to the side of the stage and took a seat which gave the best view of the row of tables set up for the remaining contestants. One couple had already been eliminated and the remaining contestants were Jenny & Tina and a father and son team. At the moment they were level pegging in points. Everything now depended on how well the contestants performed in this round.

The contestants were now dressed in white overalls with navy and white striped aprons. White hats covered their hair. The clock was set for five minutes. The ticking louder than ever it appeared, started when each contestant was ready and positioned behind their benches.

The first giggles rang out as each contestant tried (red faced) to attach the length of skin casing to the nozzle end of the sausage machine. It wasn't too difficult to guess what was going through the minds of the audience members as the stuffing process was attempted many times. Bruce's eyes were watering as he tried in vain to suppress his own giggles and remain in control. Pretty soon it all became too much and he laughed as loud as everyone else and had to turn away briefly from the scene before him. He loved this show so much; as to his way of thinking; there was no greater sound than that of laughter. Though he worked hard and managed to make it look effortless the show was a real joy to be part of and he loved it. The clock seemed to sound ever louder as it ticked away. The second hand moved jerkily around the clock as time marched on towards the end of the round.

Once more the buzzer sounded and the contestants stepped away from their tables. The butcher came forward and examined the sausages in turn and scored each contestants efforts. He picked up the not so perfect links of strangely shaped, almost (obscenely filled) casings. When some of the sausage meat spilled out of an unknotted length of casing the audience laughed as one and the sound was so deafening it was impossible to hear the butcher's scores.

Eventually Bruce called for order and the laughter became gradually less audible. There were suppressed giggles a plenty and once more the cameraman pointed the lens at certain audience members and it was a joy to see so many genuinely happy faces. The scores were added up by Bruce's assistant a very pretty blonde haired young woman.

To Tina and Jenny's surprise and delight Bruce announced that they were the winners. They shook hands with the father and son team who congratulated them on a very well deserved victory. Their sausage links had been as near perfect as you could expect.

Jenny was picked to sit in the hot seat and memorise the selection of prizes paraded on the conveyor belt as it rolled past. She had a good memory and had no doubt there would be no problem listing the prizes at the end of the show. The double doors swung open and the first prize to come through was a large chocolate gateaux. Jenny thought it very odd. She had expected a colour television, clock radio, electric kettle, or a fancy hair drier. Next a large box of chocolates appeared and passed by seemingly right under her nose. Next it was the turn of a massive deliciously golden crusted pork pie to move along the conveyor belt, the pie smelt heavenly. A crisp skinned roast chicken on a tray surrounded by golden crispy potatoes, roast parsnips and baton carrots with a tasty looking mound of stuffing rolled by on the conveyor belt. The sumptuous aroma of food caused her nostrils to twitch with sheer pleasure. Next a plate of custard tarts rolled by, followed by a dish of thick soft whipped dairy ice cream studded with toffee pieces with a delicate pile of wafers set out on a serving tray.

Jenny could sit still no longer! The temptingly mouth-watering dishes had the desired effect on her senses. Saliva practically flowed from her mouth. It was sheer torture seeing all that wonderful food just drifting by almost within her reach, she must have something to eat. The hunger pangs became almost unbearable as her taste buds lit up like the bulbs on a pinball machine. She would reach out and make a grab for one of the wonderful dishes, sink her teeth into a roast chicken or relish the taste of a juicy golden crusted pork pie. She would savour the flavour of smooth rich creamy custard tart. She could almost sense the taste of rich dairy ice cream with toffee pieces spread out invitingly on a delicate crispy wafer.

The temptation all became too much and she tried to lunge forward and grab one of the wonderfully filled dishes. To her horror she found it impossible to move her arms. Suddenly her eyes blinked open. She found herself standing in front of the open door of the fridge. She had been trying in vain to reach inside and grab a custard tart. Just before her fingers reached the tart to pick it up, a loud voice called out.

'Put that back!'

Guiltily she stepped back and closed the fridge door. Her mum put a comforting arm around her daughter's shoulders and steered her away from temptation.

Reincarnation

I couldn't believe my luck when the envelope slipped through the letterbox and dropped on to my welcome mat in the hall. Psychic Monthly runs competitions on a regular basis. For   example the prizes mainly consist of, a voucher for a free palm reading, or a tarot card session.

Now and again there's a one night stay in a haunted mansion, if you have the desire to be literally scared out of your wits! This month's prize is the most amazing, awesome, never before seen or heard of, tip; top; totally out of this world and one time ever chance; to reincarnate the one person you ever dreamed of interviewing. The only stipulation is that there can be no personal ties to the soul you wish to reincarnate. You get the chance to spend one whole hour asking all the questions you have ever dreamed of.

With my fingers shaking almost uncontrollably, I picked up the envelope and without finesse ripped it open and pulled out the leaflet with a card attached. My excitement levels were so high I actually jumped up and down several times shouting.

'Oh wow, wow, wow, this is just fantastic! Yippee!'

This one off, totally top-tastic prize is mine. Thoughts zoomed into overdrive but I needed to calm down, and read the instruction leaflet as well as the details on the reverse of the prize card.

 It's of the utmost importance that the procedures stated are followed to the letter. I have been presented with a power of such magnitude that it's imperative any decision made by me is not taken lightly. I read the leaflet and instructions printed on the card several times and the one phrase that remains imprinted on my mind is as follows. It is with great pleasure that I Jenny Jakes (Editor in Chief of Psychic Monthly) present you with this most unique prize. Just one note of caution, read the instructions attached very carefully indeed!

I read the set of instructions at least a dozen times then placed the card and leaflet on my dining room table. I'd already chosen the person to reanimate or reincarnate, to use the proper term. It was only now having won the most amazing prize ever, the full enormity of the immense power within my grasp was realised. I decided to give myself a full twenty four hours to come to terms with this awesome power and totally unique opportunity. My state of mind was much too excitable to handle such immense power. It would be all too easy to make a mistake and goodness knows what the consequences would be!

Difficult though it was I spent that extraordinary day going about my normal daily routine. Living as ordinary a life as possible considering what was about to take place on the following day.

I was awake at 6 o'clock in the morning eager to discover what the day held in store for me. I'd experienced strange dreams during the night, but that wasn't unusual. I often woke up weary after spending a night drifting from one dream scenario to the next. I showered, dressed, and enjoyed tea and hot buttered toast. Shortly after the things were cleared away from my dining room table. I kept the table polished to a high sheen, the sun shone through the open slats of the window blinds bathing the room in sunlight.

I picked up my mobile phone and prized off the back section then removed the SIM card. I then peeled the SIM card from the back of the instruction leaflet and inserted it into my phone with fingers slightly shaky from both the feeling of fear and great excitement. The task completed, I placed the back section onto the phone and hesitated for a long drawn out moment. I was conscious of the change in my breathing pattern and willed myself to calm down and eventually relax!

One more time I read through the set of instructions carefully, then hesitated briefly before pressing the seven digit number code into my mobile phone. Several almost heart stopping seconds later, the dial tone finally kicked in. It seemed an eternity had passed until I heard a pleasant sounding female on the other end of the line.

'Celestial Call Centre, Daphne speaking. How may I help you?'

I was so taken aback by her words, my voice had temporarily shut down! Daphne now somewhat perturbed repeated her question. Was she an angel? I breathed in deeply filling my lungs then exhaled slowly feeling more relaxed, yet still my voice sounded a little creaky as I answered her!

'Good morning Daphne. My name is Bridie and I've won the first prize in a competition run by Psychic Monthly magazine. By the way, if you don't mind me asking are you really speaking to me from heaven or is it somewhere else…?'

The sentence soon trailed away. There was complete silence for a moment then Daphne spoke again.

'If you have this phone number then you also have a set of instructions to follow so please stick to the rules and do not ask me any more questions. Press (1), if it's a general enquiry, (2) for reincarnation or, (3) for a special intention.'

I re-read my instructions leaflet for the umpteenth time and held my breath for a second, my index finger hovered just above the numbers on the phone. I knew very well it was the number (2) that I needed to press, but my hesitation was perfectly understandable. Considering the present circumstances I found myself in, the consequences of making a mistake did not bear thinking about! Once more Daphne spoke up.

'Please be advised that whichever service you require, there may be a slight time delay in receiving an answer to your call. I will have to place you on hold until the queue is dispelled. Thank you for phoning the Celestial Call Centre! Have a wonderful day!'

I quickly pressed button (2) and to my astonishment a loud rendition of the song 'Fire', by the Animals started to play, the volume was almost deafening! Could this be a clue as to the location of the number I had just dialled? My concerns quickly evaporated when that particular tune came to an end and 'Millennium' was the next song blaring down the phone line. Once more I managed to control my breathing, even so it was somewhat laboured under the circumstances. After what seemed like hours later the music stopped playing. A male voice with a cut glass accent answered my call.

'Good morning this is the Reincarnation Enquiry Service who is the person you wish to interview?'

'I would really like to speak to Kenneth Williams if that's possible?'

'I have to ask you the appropriate questions as a security measure you understand. I take it you have your instruction leaflet close to hand. If everything is in order we will be able to transport Kenneth directly to your home in a very short while.'

The questions were straight forward and I answered each one rapidly without a moments' hesitation as stated on the leaflet in a clear voice to avoid any misunderstanding. After all having come this far I didn't want to jeopardise my chance of interviewing one of my favourite film stars of all time.

'Thank you for your patience; all is in order and you can expect your visitor presently.'

The call came to an abrupt end and suddenly I was aware of the total silence in my home. Before I had the chance for another thought a brilliant white light appeared. It filled the whole of one wall in my dining room. Seconds later a portal appeared and gradually the opening revealed a door which opened before my astonished gaze. Kenneth Williams appeared from the other side and stepped through the open door and straight into my dining room. The blood drained away so fast from my head I almost fainted. He took one look at me and called out in a very whining, irritated tone of voice.

'Here what's your game? I'm supposed to be having my eternal rest! Mind you it's not much of one now. Oh no! Most of the Carry On team are busily crowding my section of the afterlife! Dropping like flies they are!'

'Hello Kenneth or should I call you Mr Williams?'

'That'll be Mr Williams to you. Who are you anyway? I'll have you know I was having a game of celestial billiards against Bernard Bresslaw! When all of a sudden puff: my balls dropped out of my control and here I am. What do you want anyway?'

'I'm so sorry to have disturbed your game. But you see, the thing, is I won first prize in Physic Monthly magazine. The winner gets to reincarnate your favourite actor, or any other person you really want to meet who has now passed on, and I chose you. This once in a lifetime or should I say afterlife opportunity, to interview a member of the deceased was just too amazing to ignore. I chose you Mr Williams because you're my favourite star of the Carry On films. Please don't be angry with me, one hour is nothing really compared to eternity.'

He smiled then and took a seat opposite mine at the table. His facial expression changed to one of smug superiority and his voice modulated to an upper crust tone.

'Well my dear this is an honour; for you I mean! It's not everyday someone like you gets to meet a star of my calibre. Let us proceed with the interview then shall we? Hold on for a moment would you! I'll just turn my head slightly so you can see my best side!'

He gave a haughty but dignified chuckle. His facial expression changed on hearing my first question. He looked down his nose as if a bad smell had just been detected.

'Why is it Mr Williams that in most of your films you manage to lose control of your trousers and they end up falling around your ankles?'

Once more his expression changed completely as did his voice. His performance was brilliant as he did a perfect impression of Monsieur Camembert, the character he played in (Carry On. Don't Lose Your Head).

'Not that it's any of your business: but dropping the trousers was written into my contract. I received royalties from a famous underwear manufacturer every time I flashed me boxers, now what do you think of that!'

It was a statement rather than a question. He smiled mischievously with a real glint in his eye and to my delight winked at me in a friendly manner.

'Is it true that you and Sid James didn't get really get on that well?'

His expression and voice totally transformed yet again. He now sounded just like Arthur the Caterpillar from (Will 'o' the Wisp).

'Well I must say there wasn't that much of a friendship between us. He was forever casting aspersions if you understand my meaning! With a complexion like a pickled walnut, who was he to judge?'

Once again he did not require an answer. An extremely loud cackle escaped his lips. Then his features became composed into a relaxed demeanour. Before my eyes his face transformed into the now familiar aristocratic appearance.

'Thank you for being so frank. Now about your diary I wondered why you decided to write the entries in several different handwriting styles.'

'That's an easy one to answer. The simple truth is I was just showing off. If you've done your research you will know I was trained as an engraver. That meant I needed to be able to produce many styles of handwriting, plain, roman, gothic, copperplate and Uncle Tom Cobbley and all!'

He giggled at that. Then carried on talking.

'It was more than just about showing off. I knew that one day the diaries would come to light and felt it would be hilarious to leave a mystery to confuse and perplex the great and the good. I suspect they thought me to be a victim of multiple personality disorder. But the fact of the matter is that I was just exceedingly talented.'

He laughed out loud at that. I could feel a giggle start in my stomach and it worked its way up and blasted through my lips and manifested as a great big, joyful, brilliant laugh. We both looked at each other and carried on laughing until a great ball of light appeared once more filling every bit of space on the dining room wall. The time with him was over all too soon. I wanted to shake his hand but wasn't too sure about the etiquette involved when it came to members of the deceased. We gave each other a knowing wink and cheery wave. He turned and stepped through the portal. The door closed behind him. The fissure became dull then disappeared. I was left wondering how on earth it could all have been possible.

I had a sudden thirst and went into the kitchen. I headed straight for the kettle and filled it at the tap. I popped a teabag in my favourite mug and one teaspoon of sugar.

I headed back into the now empty dining room. I picked up the phone, leaflet, card and envelope and brought them into the kitchen placing them on the table. My mind was busier than a factory in full production. I knew that this past hour had not been a dream, but a reality. As that thought flashed into my brain something strange occurred.

The envelope promptly turned to dust then disappeared. The same thing happened to the card and leaflet. I picked up my phone and realised with certainty, before I even removed the back panel that the SIM card would also be gone. I placed my own SIM card back in the phone, just at that moment the kettle boiled. I brewed a mug of tea and sat at the table in my kitchen. Just then

I heard the beeping sound of a text message being delivered. I picked up the phone and my eyes lit up in amazement. As I read the message laughter bubbled up inside me once more. I knew without doubt that my encounter with Kenneth Williams had indeed really taken place as the phrases flashed up on my mobile screen.

'Ooh I do feel queer.'

'You can be as wude as you like matron.'

'I was once a weak man. But once a week's enough for any man.'

'Stop messing about.'

The text ended just as his diary had, when the last entry was written the night he died.

'What's the bloody point?'

Three smiley faces accompanied that last message. I whispered a reply to him.

'Rest in peace Kenneth thanks for the laughs.'

Salvation

It was Christmas Eve once again and the bitter cold seeped into my limbs with a dreadful bone numbing icy chill. I rubbed my hands together enthusiastically, in a vain attempt to start the blood flowing again in order to thaw my frozen finger tips. The falling snow was swiftly settling down on the ground changing the pavements, from a uniform dull grey to pristine white. There was no likelihood of preventing the gush of thick flurries of snow dancing wildly through the air stirring to a tune which remained inaudible to human hearing.

Every single year since joining the organisation, I counted it my privilege to volunteer for duty on this particular night. My fellow Salvation Army Branch members were full of praise for such generosity. My choosing to work this shift in particular, allowed another member to relish the chance to enjoy an evening off. Usually it was someone with a young family who counted themselves fortunate to stay at home, and help prepare for the big day ahead.

In the early evening our chapel had been packed to full capacity with people. Each and every person intent on celebrating the Christmas prayer service, followed by joyfully enthusiastic voices singing Carols. Now the service had come to an end. The congregation full of Christmas spirit had dispersed after the traditional greetings and gone their separate ways.

The time had come for those of us who were on duty this Christmas Eve night; to ensure the soup tureens were filled and the urns replenished with freshly brewed tea and coffee. When that task was completed the urns and tureens were loaded onto the several vans   our headquarters were lucky enough to own. Our mission as always was to seek out the homeless; the vagrants and tramps, alcoholics, drug addicts and those purely unlucky souls who found themselves through no fault of their own, without any form of shelter from the bitterly cold night. It was our duty to offer a cup of soup, or a hot drink and a kind word to ward off the chill and desperate loneliness for just a brief moment.

It was a surprise to myself on realisation that twenty five years had passed since I had walked into this actual branch ready and willing to enlist in God's own infantry regiment. It was our task to do whatever we could in order to save the sick, the lonely, and the down and outs, who wandered through the doors needing help. There had been no hesitation on my part when asked to sign the pledge abstaining from alcohol. Excessive amounts of alcohol had in the past, and now in the present day caused the ruin of many a life.

My rank of which I was immensely proud was that of Major. I had worked diligently in order to rise up the ladder and attain promotion. Being an officer would have allowed me to omit some of the more unsavoury tasks that the job entailed. This was even more evident on the night duties. But in truth my main reason for joining and devoting my life to the Salvation Army, was in order to be always in constant contact with the down at heel. Especially when it came to alcoholics. It was my duty and indeed my soul vocation in life to offer each and every one of them salvation.

My thoughts return briefly to the long ago days of my childhood. My mother I remember well was so very beautiful. Her looks were those a movie star would envy and her heart was the kindest you could ever imagine. She was quick to spot the good in all and sadly blind when it came to recognising the bad in anyone. Her nature was such that she would willingly forgive any misdemeanour, or pain caused by others. You often hear of people with hearts of gold and in her case it was especially true. That generosity of heart was to prove the cause of her downfall.

My father, the total opposite of my mother was a permanently angry man. He grudgingly doled out the bare minimum of housekeeping money with which to feed and clothe his wife and their four children. How often had I seen her carefully count out the money from an almost empty purse? Deep lines caused by constant worry were etched on her beautiful features. It wasn't difficult for me to understand her dread, of being more often than not unable to make ends meet. She knew it would be pointless to ask my father for more money. The money he did earn, was mainly kept for himself. Leaving him free to spend it on his first love, which in his case was alcohol.

Friday and Saturday nights he returned home from the pub blind drunk, extremely angry, always in the mood for a fight. My mother was like a nervous bird flapping around all evening unable to settle. Hoping and praying in the terror she experienced, that he would mercifully pass out on his arrival home. More often than not before the weekend was over he would have viciously lashed out with his fists inflicting bruises or a black eye.

When I grew a little older and became stronger my protectiveness towards my mother came to the fore. The first night when I confronted my father head on he beat the hell out of me before swearing.

'Don't ever try that again Frank you little bastard, or I will make sure to break your bleeding neck.'

It was well worth the punishment I endured to save my mother from his fists for once.

The Christmas when I was thirteen years old was the worst one of my whole life. Even now the memory of it is burned like a brand and causes me as much pain. As usual my mother was left scrimping to buy even the basics of food, and a selection of small inexpensive gifts to give to her children. Our next door neighbours' house had been burgled just days before Christmas. It wasn't as if they had anything much to steal. Unknown to my father they had been invited to share Christmas dinner with our family; even though there wasn't much to spare.

That particular Friday night my father came home drunk but surprisingly much earlier than usual. Mrs Allen knocked the door soon after. My mother invited her in saying.

'Come in Tina I'll make you a cup of tea!'

'What time do you want us to come for dinner on Christmas Day Ellen?'

As soon as the words were spoken my father leaped from his armchair and grabbed my mother by the arm. He squeezed her skin in a vice like grip, in pain the tears sprang unbidden from her eyes.

'Who do you think you are asking people to my house for a free meal? You don't earn a bloody penny. All you own is down to me, from the clothes on your back to the roof over your head, you ungrateful bitch and don't you dare ever forget it!'

Mrs Allen made a lunge towards him trying to loosen his grip away from my mother's arm. He landed a vicious punch slamming his fist into her face. Blood spurted from a cut above Tina's eye. The poor woman fled the house calling out.

'Don't worry Ellen I'll get Jack to sort him out, the drunken bullying bastard!'

At that point my father grabbed mother by the throat with both hands and squeezed with mounting pressure until it seemed her eyes would pop out. Each one of their four children set on him trying in vain to get him to loosen his grip and set her free. The sheer insanity of his blinding rage gave him strength of almost superhuman proportions. He flung us across the whole length of the room one by one as if swatting away annoying insects.

The four of us screamed and begged for him to please stop hurting her, please leave her alone. Our cries and pleas fell on deaf ears! Soon the tears of helplessness turned first to that of anger then wild despair, at being powerless to do anything which would save our mother's life.

The blood quickly drained from her lovely face leaving her complexion grey and mask like in appearance. The light in her eyes dimmed until there was no spark left. Her eyelids briefly fluttered like broken butterfly wings before coming to rest on her lifeless cheeks. Ellen took one final gasp before she slumped to the floor lying motionless like a rag doll. At last her husband had loosened his grip on her neck, but it was far too late!

Jack and Tina Allen rushed through the door just in time to watch my mothers' body hit the floor! Their faces mirrored that of each other, drained of colour knowing they could do nothing. An ambulance was called but we all knew they could not save her. The lifeless corpse was already growing cold. Jack Allen phoned the Police. My father was arrested and later charged with murder and sentenced to spend the rest of his miserable life in prison.

My thoughts return to the present. I still have some tasks to complete before my shift is over for the night. I park the van close to the viaduct. This is one of the main locations where the homeless, drug addicts and alkies usually gather together, setting up their makeshift camp underneath the shelter of the tall arches. I set up a wooden trestle table, then place the soup tureens and tea and coffee urns side by side. The plastic cups and bread rolls are set out on a tray with a couple of sprigs of holly, it is Christmas Eve after all. One of the soup tureens has a red sticker placed strategically out of sight. I fill the plastic cups, my warm and friendly smile never slipping for a second. I hand them out in turn to the flotsam and jetsam of humanity surrounding me, some looking forlorn, desperately sad, or just plain out of it due to how much strong alcohol or illegal drugs they have managed to swallow.

Tomorrow morning the police will be sure to find several lifeless bodies underneath the viaduct, or within close proximity to that area. There will be the odd few corpses lying around here and there, all along the main route I will take tonight. Who will bother to investigate the deaths of these vagrants? Who among these lost souls have anyone left who cares about them? Who among them is lucky enough to have a place to call their own?

Many people will die on this Christmas Eve night. Cases of hypothermia are not unexpected in these low temperatures. Those unfortunates who have died on these snow laden streets will be briefly pitied, but soon forgotten. Their untimely but not unexpected deaths will be attributed to their lifestyle finally catching up with them.

I admit to having played my part and have never felt any guilt because of it. Alcoholics ruin the lives of not just themselves, but those who are closest to them; their families and friends. I am fulfilling a vital service to humanity by offering them (Salvation) albeit of my own choosing.

A few less alcoholics will disappear from the streets, unable to cause any more trouble and heartache. Some drug addicts will have had their last fix. Just one cup of my own special recipe soup is all that's required. There is no suffering involved. Death comes swiftly and the process is painless. You could say it was the humane thing to do really; putting an end to the misery of their wasted lives.

The tall impressive figure blends perfectly into the shadows with the skill of a chameleon. His intense observation is centred on the frail form of an elderly man lying motionless in the bed. The man's energy levels are now depleting at considerable speed. His life force is rapidly dwindling to the same extent grains of golden sand pour through the glass funnel of an egg timer.

Charles is all too aware his condition is terminal. He's also become resigned to the basic fact his life will soon be over. Despite this knowledge, he's content as it's humanly possible to be under the circumstances. Mercifully the severity of pain has lessened, the medication has been altered sufficiently to bring it under control. He suffers only minor symptoms of discomfort, but laments the helplessness of his weak and feeble body!

The hospice staff are experts in palliative care. The concern and compassion received since his admittance has more than restored his faith in the empathy of human beings.

It's now 3 o' clock in the morning. One swift glance at the florescent dial confirms this fact. He insisted on having this particular clock placed by his bedside. He's unable to wear a watch anymore because his wrists are so fragile the skin bruises easily; it would be much too uncomfortable. It remains of the utmost importance to him, that day or night the passage of time can be registered. He's unable to sleep, in truth he has no desire to lose consciousness. It's imperative to savour every single second of the life span remaining.

In the room devoid of light he sees virtually nothing but the clock dial: yet there is an awareness fermenting in his subconscious mind. He practically senses the grim reaper waiting in the wings, concealed in the shadows. Patient and soundless the angel of death waits for his cue, before his presence on stage signals the final curtain call.

Suddenly the intruder senses the dying man is unlike anyone he has ever been in contact with. His brain capacity is immense! This knowledge leaves him disconcerted! Even more unsettling is the absolute certainty, that the elderly man has become aware of his presence in the shadows. The odds of a human being possessing the brain power to tune into one of his kind are without doubt countless! This person is exceptional! The being concealed in the shadows is astounded by the knowledge and enormously intrigued to discover more about this remarkable man.

Charles understanding of the hidden being is becoming ever more apparent as the seconds tick past. It's not only his awareness of the being concealed in the shadows that has him startled. A sudden intuition forms a name flashing neon like in his brain. The name (Frouros) is fashioned in letters so enormous they completely fill the wide screen of his mind. A (eureka) moment of blinding clarity registers the implication of the ancient Greek word. This word translates as (Sentinel).

Intense joy warms his heart for a few precious seconds before the feeling is rapidly replaced by fear of the unknown. At long last after a lifetime of meticulous research can it actually be true… The train of thought comes to an abrupt halt. His capacity to breath is suddenly depleted. He reaches out for the oxygen mask, inhaling anxiously until his lungs are once more filled with air. His heart rate slows to an even rhythm.

His gaze is once more drawn to the clock by his side. Time may be running out much faster than he would have wished; yet it was still of such vital importance; more so now than during the whole of his life. Tomorrow had already begun! There was no guarantee that he would survive long enough to see the light of dawn, never mind an entire day.

(Frouros). The being hidden from Charles sight, now acknowledges the unspoken word. With a brain capacity of infinite magnitude there is little difficulty reading the minds of humans. It would take as little effort as reading the words of a printed page. The spilt second Charles thinks of a word it registers immediately in the mind of (Frouros the Sentinel). Frouros has linked in to Charles on every level now, not just his thoughts, nor his senses, but every single nerve and blood cell throughout the body of this dying man. Each and every sensation is experienced to the full. The deterioration of the body's cells; the pain blocked by morphine, the loss of signals from the brain to the nerve endings. The sluggish course of life blood flowing through arteries and veins is registered in the mind and body of Frouros.

He shudders in horror at the extreme and powerful awareness of the dying human being. Throughout all these centuries as a gatherer, it has never occurred to him to wonder what it meant to be human!

His and many others existence depended on harvesting the energy generated by living beings. He has spent over a thousand years travelling in pursuit of gathering the life force of billions of humans, animals and all other sources available. Alien beings of his type belonging to the (Frouros), devote their entire lives to harvesting energy which is then taken back to their home planet. Until now he has never before thought to make use of his vast power; in order to discover what the process of dying actually entails. This new awareness is not one he relishes experiencing. The whole process of dying is abhorrent and leads him to reflect on his own mortality.

Though beings of his kind have an average life span far in excess of human beings. At the very least their kind can expect to exist for 5000 years, but they are not immortal! Their physiology is vastly different from humans. They are much more sophisticated and highly superior to human beings. This is partly due to the length of time they have existed in order to evolve to such a greater extent. In appearance though they bear a close resemblance to humanoids the distinctions are immediately apparent. They are taller than human beings, standing at least 8 feet in height. Their skin tone is of a metallic golden hue and their hair is of the lightest shade of blonde, almost white. They have amazing distinctive amber tinted eyes, almost feline in appearance. They possess remarkable sight, which enables them to see as clearly in the dark as they do in daylight.

The planet they originate from is appropriately named Creator, their existence marks the point of creation which has been eternal. They have always been present, their existence had no beginning and there will be no end. The level of intelligence they possess would be inconceivable to the majority of human beings. Scientists from their planet created the universe as we know it. The vast galaxy of planets and stars contains an infinite source of energy, to be harvested in perpetuity. The energy sources existence is to maintain the planet and the lives of its inhabitants. The technology of invisible cloaking devices does actually exist! It was developed by the planet's scientists, to enable their gigantic circular star ships to travel throughout the galaxy virtually undetected.

Billions of years previously Earth commenced as a vast experiment in the creation of new life. An experiment that succeeded way beyond the expectations of the Creators. The environmental conditions on Earth were so perfected the planet produced not just one life form, but a myriad of species providing abundant sources of energy. Each life force can be harvested at the split second before death. The Frouros gather energy sources from stars, planets, humans and any other species with a life force. When a star becomes depleted of energy and eventually dies, it becomes a red giant and expels the outer layers of gas dimming gradually to darkness. It remains in orbit but can no longer be seen. Stars and planets die but new ones are continually created to replace them.

Over many millennia, there have been a very few accidental breeches of secrecy. Some human beings have glimpsed the Frouros themselves, or caught sight of their vast star ships. The accounts of these sightings have given an element of truth to the stories handed down over the centuries of God like creatures and flying saucers. The famous Nazka lines are not from imagination but based on real sightings of beings from the far reaches of outer space. In the case of star ship sightings these were due to the decrease in energy levels, essential to maintain the cloaking devices.

In 15th century England the so called 'myth' of the grim reaper came into being. Rumours of the skeleton in a black hooded robe, carrying a scythe spread like wild fire, and chilled the hearts of all who heard the story. Yet in reality the Frouros bear no resemblance to the terrible creature, conjured up in the mind of that terrified witness to their existence. Right across the world in almost every country, myths and legends began in the distant past. These legends first recorded on stone tablets, then written on sacred scrolls, later printed in books and narrated in fables have both delighted and struck fear in the human race.

Charles senses the intrusion of the Frouros. He has no energy in which to expel the powerful being, who is invading every corner of his body and mind. The only source of power left to him is that of his brain and he concentrates thought directly to the mind of the intruder. Frouros is astonished at the power of mind from a weak and dying man. He relinquishes control over Charles and breaks the link. The respite of not having to bear the pain and decay of the dying human is palpable. He is shaken to his very core by the brief experience of human suffering and the knowledge of what it means to be mortal.

For the brief time they were melded together in mind and body Charles glimpsed the essence of this powerful being. The experience is one he has longed for throughout the whole of his life. So many questions unanswered, yet in this brief connection insight begins. There is so much more than he could ever have imagined. He must see Frouros before it's too late! Surely he will provide answers to at least some of the questions Charles has pondered for all these years!

Frouros has never imagined what being human entailed. That question has never arisen in the thousand years of his own existence. His entire purpose in life is to gather the life force of the dying. He has never given a thought for the feelings of the humans, animals, or any other species. He has given no thought to what happens to stars and planets drained of energy until there is nothing left. Suddenly he has become aware that there are so many questions only Charles can answer.

He dispenses with the chameleon like camouflage and steps from the shadows. Charles hears the footsteps of the being walking across the room. He reaches out, clicks on the light switch. The room is now flooded with light. He stares in astonishment at the sight of the tall figure now standing at the foot of his bed. The Gods of legend are not a myth but stark reality. The proof of which stands before him in a being both powerful and majestic. Frouros speaks for the first time and Charles is overawed by the richness of his voice.

'You realise it would be much easier Charles to communicate telepathically, but I feel you wish to hear my voice, it's a human trait. You know that time is running out. It's astonishing that you also recognise who I am. You are the first life form I have ever encountered to have sensed my presence. All your questions will be answered. There is no need to worry if you have enough time left. There is so much I also need to know, only you can give me the answers so you understand we can help each other.'

Charles feels overwhelmed by the emotion of this encounter. The experience is something he could never have imagined in his wildest dreams. Silent tears slide down his cheeks in twin rivulets, not of sadness but pure joy. The being walks around to the side of the bed and lowers his body onto a chair. Instinctively he reaches for the hand of the dying man already his knowledge of the human psyche is considerable. The decision has not been taken lightly to make use of his power to suspend the process of time!

What seems like an age passes before the hands of the clock once more move forward. Just before the light of dawn appears the last grain of sand slips down the imaginary glass funnel. The pooled knowledge has now enlightened both parties. Charles bears no animosity towards the being who will now drain away his life force. It's a simple and unavoidable fact of life that we each have a time limit and Charles is ready to let go.

Frouros lays an open hand lightly on the dying man's shoulder. A stream of silver vapour arises from the body and swirls round forming a perfect sphere. He steps away from the empty vessel now lying motionless in the bed. His gaze is drawn in wonder at the orb grasped in his hands. The very essence of everything that was Charles is now contained in this precious silver sphere.

It will be many years before Frouros returns to his home planet. The store of energy will increase over time until the vast containers aboard his star ship are filled to capacity. The one single silver orb containing the life force of Charles will not be added to the container just yet! Frouros will study the essence of this man until every fact about him is learned. Then he will truly understand what it means to be human!

On that fateful day just a few short months ago; I remember distinctly that it hadn't been my idea to choose (The Book). To be honest and it may sound strange; somehow (The Book) carefully selected me to be its next owner! My thoughts reversed down memory lane to the not too distant past.

It was proving an impossible task at that time to find a new job having been made redundant. The company I worked for had been bankrupted and the premises sold off. On that particular day to my dismay, the contents of my purse amounted to the not so grand total of just £2. Now it seemed a real possibility that I would be kicked out of the flat which was my home. The rent arrears had mounted up and my bank account was nearly depleted, what was left would not scratch the surface of the debt I had acquired.

I found myself wandering the streets aimlessly first thing on that fateful Saturday morning. A troubled soul deep in thought wondering how I would ever manage to keep the roof above my head. My legs transported me forward automatically seeming to know where I was headed. I allowed them to propel me onwards uncaring where they may lead. My mind was in turmoil speculating as to how I was going to overcome the pressing problem of settling my debts. How was I going to secure employment in order to make ends meet? Most importantly how was I going to find enough money to buy food? The gnawing in my belly could not be ignored!

Abruptly my steps halted of their own volition. I found myself standing in front of a shop window staring at the poster which read 'Second Hand Book Sale'. Reading is without question one of my favourite hobbies. I couldn't resist the urge to go and browse through the stacks of books which awaited inside the shop. It was an irresistible opportunity to put my worries to one side for a few precious minutes.

Slowly I meandered along the rows of trestle tables, each one held books of every genre stacked in neat piles. There were Murder Mystery's arranged next to Historical Novels. Thrillers placed against Westerns: Self Help Manuals vying for space with a range of Recipe Books. There were Books of Dream Interpretations. Books of Adventure Stories, Travel Guides, Books of Mysterious Treasures and volumes of Encyclopaedias, plus a whole myriad of other exciting subjects.

 Each and every single book was packed with wonderful facts or just brilliantly fascinating stories waiting patiently to be read. All the books lingered just waiting for someone to choose them. To hold the book in their hands turn the page and begin to read the first few lines; before the decision was made as to whether this was the one to buy and take home.

It was a fanciful train of thought but I imagined each book as having some type of awareness. Some of the books displayed front covers which were so attractive you felt compelled to pick them up in order to study every minute detail of the artwork. Some books were bound in leather. These books had the power to attract the potential buyer to pick them up and breathe in the aroma of natural hide. Sometimes people briefly glimpsed the contents of first pages though not always. The substance of each book promised the reader everything they could ever desire. From the most exhilarating of great adventures, to poignant love stories, to the greatest murder mysteries.

Books provided an insight into the study of the world, or the science of space travel. History, Geography and Science. How to cook the most delicious dishes, the study of crafts, such as sketching, painting or perhaps even, the intricate and fragile art of origami. Books are the genuine treasures of this world and hold the key to filling our minds with dreams and ambitions.

Each and every book contains something amazing to recommend it. They lie in wait silent and stationary! But they are oh so very eager to be picked up, to be held. They want to be bought, taken home, read and cherished; for as long as it would take the reader to turn each page avidly until the very last word of their story were told, or each written instruction was absorbed. I fancied my imagination which remained always so vivid was working overtime, in order to force the worries and woes of life into a tiny dark corner of my subconscious. Once inside that recess all would be forgotten for a brief respite.

I sauntered to the very last trestle table at the far end of the shop briefly pausing when a loud buzzing sound was heard, the location of which seemed to be close at hand. A great stack of books to my right which had toppled over in a heap seemed to be where the noise was coming from. The sound ever louder drew me to that table. I began rummaging through the pile of books in order to discover the source of the sound, similar to a number of bees buzzing in unison. An idea popped into mind that somebody had already been rifling fervently among the great pile of books previously. Maybe there had been a search for a mobile phone which had slipped from a pocket or a bag. Maybe the buzzing sound was in fact a ring tone. The books were in such a state of disarray.

An unfamiliar tingling sensation ran along my fingers as I cleared books from the top of the pile. As my hands brushed fleetingly against the surface of each book the tingling sensation intensified dramatically. At last I picked up a leather bound volume the sensation ceased as suddenly as it had begun. I examined the large leather bound book thoroughly it was impossible to find a title or even the authors name. As I continued to peer intensely something strange began to occur. Golden printed letters appeared on the leather cover, they danced before my very eyes darting this way and that as if unsure how to form themselves into the precise order. My thoughts suddenly focused on my immediate worries. I was desperate for help in order to solve my predicament nothing short of a miracle was called for. I closed my eyes tightly and made a silent but fervent wish. When I opened them again the golden letters had formed themselves into a title.

Everything You Need.

I could hardly believe my eyes it seemed the book had read my thoughts and created the title in response to my wish. I glanced at the price tag it was just £2. I realised that couldn't possibly be right. The book was bound in fine leather and appeared to be antiquated judging by its appearance. There was no justification for spending my last £2 on a book. There was no nourishment to be gained from a book. A book could never slake my thirst. I returned the leather bound volume on top of the pile.

As the thoughts wrestled within my conscience the tingling returned causing my fingertips to almost spark, it was the strangest sensation. Surely it was absurd to part with my last £2. Against all reason and struggling with my own free will I suddenly snatched up the book. The tingling sensation once more stopped abruptly. Once more I glanced at the title. The golden letters swirled around for many moments then came to a halt. This time the gold letters were rearranged into a completely different title which read.

Put Your Trust In Me.

The decision was made to purchase the book and worry about the consequences of my actions later. Walking over to the counter at the front of the shop I noticed a sign above it (Help Wanted). It was an amazing piece of luck I fervently hoped the vacancy was still on offer. A tall slim elderly white haired man with a friendly expression on his face stood behind the counter. He was smartly dressed in a dark grey suit. He wore a plain white shirt with a very flamboyantly colourful bowtie. His neat short hairstyle was immaculate not a stray hair out of place. I put the book on the counter and handed him the £2.Then asked outright.

'Is the job still on offer?'

'Yes it is. I can arrange a short interview now if you have the time to spare.'

'I have all the time in the world unfortunately and trust me this job would be a dream come true.'

'I'm about to close for lunch. Would you care to join me?'

'Thanks for the invitation but that £2 I just handed over has left me penniless.'

My face suddenly seemed far too hot for comfort. The flush in my cheeks caused them to burn bright red with embarrassment.

'It will have to be my treat then.'

He smiled at me and I couldn't have been more grateful. We walked a little way down the street in the direction of a small cafe. The wonderful aroma of freshly brewed coffee drifted through the open window. I found myself suddenly very thirsty. Once inside we made our way to a table just behind the doorway. The delightful smell of food being cooked escaped from the direction of the kitchen causing my taste buds to work overtime.

I had barely eaten all week and had just spent my last £2 on a strange and antiquated book, with not the slightest idea of its contents. Yet for some inexplicable reason my worries had already lessened considerably. As we tucked into roast chicken dinners and shared a pot of tea brewed to perfection contentment flooded through me. Mr Baines remained silent knowing my hunger and thirst were extensive.

After the meal was eaten and the last drop of tea drained from the pot my interview began. He questioned me about qualifications attained and work experience up to the present date. As luck would have it I kept a copy of my C.V. in my bag along with a file holding my certificates. I may have been at a low ebb, but was determined to be prepared on the off chance like today of spotting a job vacancy. As the interview drew to conclusion he smiled and told me the job was mine. Relief flooded through me. Still though I lacked any funds was on the point of being evicted and there were bills which must be settled. Despite these concerns the offer of work was nothing short of a miracle and I was overjoyed to have finally found employment. I had already explained my financial situation to Mr Baines, mainly the lack of any funds whatsoever!

'Miss Hart. May I call you Celia?'

I nodded my assent. He carried on the conversation.

'There is a small flat above the shop. It contains one bedroom, a kitchen, a living room and a bathroom. It's in need of a good clean and airing plus the odd coat of paint in most rooms to brighten them up. If you are willing to take on the task of sprucing it up. I will advance you the money to cover your immediate debts plus personal expenses. You can repay the loan in manageable instalments from your wages, on a weekly basis until the debt is repaid. By the way you are welcome to collect your possessions and move in today. I can assure you the rent will be nominal. Do we have an agreement?'

I stood up then reached out and hugged him, not caring if he were a complete stranger or whether it was appropriate. Tears of both joy and considerable relief sprung from my eyes and slid unbidden down my cheeks. His kindness towards me was overwhelming. He gently patted my shoulder shifted backwards and withdrew from my spontaneous embrace looking somewhat embarrassed, by my display of affection and tear streaked appearance. I apologised for my impulsive behaviour, blushing furiously yet again. He smiled his reassurance, saying.

'I can assume that will be a yes then!'

We both laughed and walked back to the book shop in companionable silence. My footsteps were considerably lighter now. The heavy burden of worry had fallen off my shoulders as a weight being lifted. This outcome leaving me a much happier person than I had been for a long time. That very same day I paid off all my bills including the rent arrears. I packed my suitcase, a large cardboard box with my few belongings and moved into the small but well equipped flat. To my eyes it looked pretty well kept, the décor bright and welcoming. Mr Baines had probably told me it needed some TLC in order to make me feel as though I were doing him a favour. My rapid change of luck was almost like a grown up fairy tale, destitute, jobless and nigh on homeless at the start of the day; the complete opposite by the end of it!

One month on I had settled comfortably into the flat and added a few personal touches to the décor by painting the bedroom walls in a shade of pale gold. The new bedding was in a contrasting colour and complimented the room perfectly. In the living room I hung curtains in deep purple velvet with gold trim, matching cushions in the same material were scattered along the sofa.

Being in the book shop was an absolute joy and didn't seem like work at all. Having always been an avid reader it was the perfect job for someone like myself. My life had totally changed and improved greatly the very second I'd purchased the leather bound antiquated book with my last £2. I had been proved right to go with my instincts. Strangely the title on the front cover of the book was constantly changing. Even more bizarrely this phenomenon didn't alarm me to the degree that it should have done. Often I would find myself pondering a question, seconds later the answer would immediately be formed in the gold lettering of the title.

To date I had been far too busy to actually read any of the book. I hadn't even lifted the cover to see what was printed on the first page. Deep down inside I knew my hectic schedule over the past month hadn't anything to do with the fact that the book so far remained firmly closed. To be perfectly honest a tiny seed of suspicion about the book's subject matter had begun to form.

Daily the seed was growing rapidly into something tangible. It came as a shock to realise my thoughts were in fact spoken out loud, when another voice interrupted my train of thought.

'Talking to yourself is one of the first signs of madness or so they say!'

I focused my gaze forward and was confronted with a pair of serpent like dark green eyes. The tall gaunt figure had a thick mane of hair which was jet black. I guessed the man's age to be around fifty. He was dressed in a very old fashioned dark suit with a pristine white shirt and red silk cravat. He wore a long black cloak which was thrown back over his left shoulder to reveal the sumptuous lining of bright red silk to match the cravat. He reminds me of the typical image of a vampire with his deathly pale skin. My thoughts ran on for a few seconds, then I had to admit first vampires can't be seen in daylight and two they are creatures of myth and legend!

'Can I help you?'

'For many years I have travelled extensively to numerous countries in my quest to seek out a very rare volume.'

'If you tell me the title of that volume I will check the stock records to see if we have a copy in the shop.'

'Now that is a question I cannot answer due to the fact this particularly rare volume has a title which changes constantly. No-one has managed to discover by which name it's actually known! All I can tell you is that it's extremely special; not just rare but unique in fact. I would be willing to pay a great deal of money for this particular item, a great deal of money indeed!'

He stared at me intently scrutinising my features. Suddenly I felt icy cold as invisible tremors ran along my spine causing me to shiver. I concentrated on the computer for a short while pretending to check the stock records. I had no intention of selling this stranger my precious book.

'I am sorry you have had another wasted journey. We definitely don't have that particular book in the shop.'

'Are you absolutely certain that you don't have it here?'

'Are you accusing me of lying sir?'

He didn't get the opportunity to answer that question. Fortunately for me Mr Baines returned from the auction house at that precise moment. He couldn't fail to notice my expression was one of concern!

'Is everything alright Celia?'

'Yes Mr Baines everything is just fine. This man is searching for a particularly rare and unique antique volume. I've assured him we don't have the book in stock.'

The strange man opposite me concentrated his cold green eyed gaze towards me. The expression on his pale face was guaranteed to instil genuine fear. He then abruptly turned away and left the shop closing the door behind him with an almighty slam. The bell above the door reverberated for ages after he left ringing incessantly. Once he was out of the shop I breathed a long slow sigh of relief. The respite I was certain would not last long. Instinct warned me he would return soon enough.

Weeks passed by and the incident of the encounter with the sinister stranger remained fresh in my memory. He hadn't returned to the book shop so far and that was a great relief. I had no desire to be in his company again. I was convinced the stranger would come back and the thought of his returning gave me cause for concern. Maybe the suggestion of threat in his voice that day he was in the shop, was more prone to my imagination than reality. Without a doubt he disbelieved me when I told him about not having the book. The malevolent expression as he stared into my eyes almost reading my mind caused me to shiver involuntarily. A tremor of ice ran the length of my spine on reliving the memory.

It was on a Saturday night and not far off midnight. I was watching a favourite DVD when the sound of chiming filtered up to my flat from the premises downstairs. Strange that the shop door bell was ringing so late at night! The door must have opened but I knew it couldn't have. The only key holders for the premises were myself and Mr Baines. Who could have entered the shop and how? I had locked and bolted the door hours ago and it was to my mind secure. Pure terror suddenly shot through me causing my hair to almost stand on end as my scalp froze. The thought of who might have broken into the shop filled me with an awful dread! I had no choice but to investigate who or what lay in wait downstairs. My phone was switched to silent then hastily pushed deep into the pocked of my jeans. I walked into the kitchen opened the cupboard door under the sink, took out the metal toolbox and selected a hammer. For some unfathomable reason I went to the living room next and picked up the book to gaze at the front cover. The gold letters swirled around rapidly and came to a sudden stop forming a new title!

Get Help

Reading the latest title gave me absolutely no comfort but those words had the desired effect and jolted me into prompt action.

I took the phone from my pocket hastily switched the sound back on and rang the police. The call thankfully was answered almost immediately and I related what was happening, I was told that policemen in a patrol car would be on their way to the shop within minutes. They advised me to sit tight locking myself in to the flat for my own safety!

I ignored the advice! I picked up the book and held it tightly in the crook of my left arm. I unlocked and opened the door of the flat then picked up the hammer feeling much more secure for having something to defend myself against the unknown intruder. I imagined it could be quite some time before the police arrived. Waiting upstairs in the flat quivering with fear was not an option for me, it was a much better idea to take action now.

The book began to emit the familiar buzzing sound which had first drawn me towards it on that fateful day some months previously. It seemed to me that a vast amount of power was beginning to generate inside the book as the buzzing sound gained in force and the volume escalated! A surge of pure energy flowed through my body, quelling the fear within by transmitting a powerful strength. Stealthily I made my way downstairs. There was no need to switch on the light. My eyes adjusted immediately to the dark. It was a revelation to find my vision was unhindered despite the pitch black of the shop floor below.

The sound of books falling on to the floor quickly drew my attention. The beam of light from a torch waived erratically back and forth creating shadows which darted along the walls and ceiling. I heard the sound of laboured breathing coming from somewhere close by. I crouched low and hid safely inside an alcove before catching sight of the tall gaunt figure just a few feet away. Recognition was instantaneous but now the figure no longer held any fear for me. I had known he would return to the shop in search of the book which was now held securely under my arm. Without warning he suddenly became still and seemed to sniff the air almost like a dog attempting to pick up a scent. It was a shock to hear his voice break through the silence!

'I knew that you had lied to me! Show yourself young woman and hand over the book. You have no idea of the power contained within! The power is limitless you could never hope to gain control of it!'

The intensity of his anger and frustration became a palpable force which flew forward from his cold green eyes like two bolts of lightning. The force of that energy sent the books flying around in a frenzy of activity. Swirling masses of volumes bolted upright from the shelves and trestle tables. They flew forward at great speed magnet like towards the strange gaunt figure; before stopping in mid-air and crashing down to the floor to fall at his feet. The book under my arm buzzed even louder with greater urgency. The energy escalated to an even great degree! Instinctively I knew the book had enough power generated and finally it was ready to be opened up. I emerged from my hiding place inside the alcove and walked towards the malevolent sinister looking figure.

'You can have the book just take it and leave. The police are on their way they will be here soon.'

The cold green eyes lit up with malevolence, pure evil emanated from the tall gaunt stranger. Eagerly he held out his hands desperate to receive the book! A smile (or grimace would be more accurate) of triumph lifting the corners of his thin bloodless lips. He drew ever closer and just before he reached me I placed the open book on the floor before him! Instantly! I retreated to the safety of the alcove. I just managed to shield my eyes, as a beam of intensely blinding white light escaped the book's pages and headed straight towards the gaunt figure who screamed in terror as it hit him full force in the chest! He collapsed to the ground writhing and screaming in agony shrivelling before my very eyes. The screams ceased abruptly the figure disappeared. A pile of dust lay on the floor where he had stood just moments earlier. The dust rose up and flew out through the door as the police entered the shop. The beam of light had dimmed and now the book slammed tight shut.

Not long after the police left the shop. I locked the door behind them and returned to my flat. Minutes later I sipped strong tea from a mug! The book was placed on the table before me as the events of the night flashed through my mind. There was no rational explanation for events I had witnessed. The book had somehow fought a battle to stay with me! The immense power it contained was not to be underestimated. Once again it remained firmly closed and silent! I picked it up and gazed once more at the ever changing title on the front cover. The gold letters had rearranged themselves and once more they read.

Everything You Need

The Day the World Changed

The day began just like any other on the 6th of June 2016. Though before that new day had come to a close the world had changed in the most extraordinary way. It would have been impossible for the inhabitants of planet earth to contemplate that at 6am precisely; the world as they knew it would undergo a total transformation. There hadn't been any prior warning of the upcoming catastrophe! The event could not have been predicted by the most prominent scientists across the globe. Nor could the transformation have been detected by the most sophisticated monitoring equipment throughout the entire planet.

Dawn broke as usual through the darkness on that day. The glorious golden sun rising slowly towards the atmosphere above sent bursts of bright light flickering along the horizon. The massive orb of blinding sunlight ascended slowly in all its' glory towards the cloudless bright blue sky above. That morning I was out very early walking along the Pen-Y-Fan at Brecon. When that glorious summer day began with the rising of the glittering sun, bathing everything it contacted in a glowing warmth. I revelled at the heat of that sun shining down on my face and closed my eyes breathing in the fresh clean air, breathing deeply to revel in the wonderful aromas of nature at its best. I came to a standstill closing my eyes and remained unmoving, statue like for what seemed an age. My imagination set free to roam! Thoughts of anything and nothing danced with wild abandon flickering across the wide screen inside my mind.

I sensed the changes happening around me though my eyes remained closed. The air became cooler, suddenly making me shiver! There was something else happening which gave me cause for alarm but was impossible to put into words. One word flashed neon like in my mind, that word was (wrong) something was seriously wrong! Gradually my eyelids flickered open. Dread engulfed me like the slither of ice cold worms in the pit of my stomach. With eyes now opened wide my heart lurched uncomfortably in my rib cage at the sight presented before me.

I twirled around in a circle my vision soaking up every inch of surrounding view before me. To my abject horror the shades of differing hues of colour had vanished from the world around me. The shock was indescribable! I ran down the hill as fast as my legs would propel me. Horror at the sight of the surroundings clouding my mind.

Once in the car I pressed the central locking button before starting the engine. I drove home concentrating all my thoughts on the journey my mind fully alert to the traffic on the road. Mercifully at this time of day there were few vehicles on the road. I decided to steer clear of the motorway and drove along the A465 from Brecon to Neath, and headed on to my home in Bridgend.

Already the colossal change in the world was beginning to have dire consequences. I switched on the radio and heard news reports of plane crashes and other disasters happening all around the planet. It wasn't just the planet earth which had been drained of all colour. Everything around me appeared in black and white; like the images in old photographs. Even my car which had once been blue now looked black. The exterior and interior dashboard, lights, indicators, upholstery now appeared as monochrome.

It was no mystery why so many aeroplanes had crashed around all over the world. The control panels and instruments on every aircraft consisted of a set of dials, switches and gauges, each and every one of which set in a myriad of colour indicators! That had been the case until 6am! When the mysterious unexplained phenomenon had occurred and somehow sucked the colour from every single thing on earth! My mind was suddenly filled with vivid images of hospitals, factories, power stations, and the motorways and railway network.

How would this impossible situation affect the efficiency of any and all monitoring   equipment in hospitals, medical facilities, and industry? Colour played such a vital part in all aspects of machinery and monitoring systems of every kind. A sudden realisation of the impact this monochrome situation would have all across the world filled me with dread!

Colour was essential to our way of life. As children we are taught to keep away from the fire because it is red hot and burns. Traffic-lights had always been an efficient way of filtering the traffic in towns and cities safely and without any danger until today that is! There was no colour amber, nor green or red, nothing to distinguish one from the other. It was impossible to work out the sequence of lights safely. I sadly observed numerous car accidents on my journey home from Brecon that morning but none thankfully serious enough to harm the drivers of the crashed vehicles! Luckily I managed to avoid any danger to my car or myself during that nerve wracking voyage to the safety of my home.

It took an hour to drive back to Bridgend and then it really made an impact on me how bleak the world had now become. The monochrome world which came into being just one hour previously had turned the entire world into a cold, bleak, miserable negative image of its past former glory. The June day was still warm but the sun was now white not the beautiful golden yellow of the dawn this very morning. The sky was no longer visible in shades of blue, violet, pink or red.

I unlocked the black front door of my house which had always cheered me with its warm bright red hue. My former beautiful red bricked house was now devoid of its vivid colour and looked most uninviting in black. I unlocked the door and stepped into the hallway of my home. The fitted carpet was no longer blue, the mahogany banister was no longer a warm shade of reddish brown. The wallpaper was no longer the sunny hue of warm tones. I walked into the kitchen were once the brightly coloured yellow walls reminded me of sunshine. Now those same walls were dull and cheerless. I ran around my home from one room to the next. First the ground floor then upstairs! Already I mourned the lack of colour and warmth of welcome in my own home. I stepped into my bathroom, pausing just long enough to take a deep breath and caught sight of my reflection in the mirror above the sink. My eyes were no longer the familiar shade of blue I was used to seeing and my once vivid red hair now looked black. My skin was almost white the pallor most unhealthy looking.

I walked down the staircase and into the living room. I switched on the radio just in time to catch the latest news broadcast. The time was now 7am. During the past 60 minutes a large percentage of the population of the world had taken to the streets of every major city across the globe. The crowds were like frightened sheep wanting to know what was happening and why. Many believed that somehow the leaders of governments worldwide must have had prior warning of the disaster which had taken place at 6 am! There were riots taking place in almost every town and city across the entire planet earth!

Just one week to the day since the world changed beyond recognition, suicides were being committed at an ever increasing and alarming rate in every country across the planet. A whole world devoid of colour had caused a significant increase in the population suffering from a series of mental disorders!

Being an artist myself it saddened me to look at the pictures I had once lovingly created in so many different hues. Now sadly every single one of those drawing and paintings   lacked any colour and it depressed me to see the dull monochrome on paper and canvas.

One month had now passed since the day the world had lost not only colour but also the natural beauty of brilliant sunrises and sunsets; the once wonderful and varied shades of flowers, plants, fish , birds and everything else which once was so beautiful to behold. The sky had turned black that fateful day and the apathy of the human race turned to sheer dread! The dread escalated to pure terror of what might happen next. For the next 7 days the sky remained black as night oppressive like a monster waiting in the darkness getting ready to emerge! The birds no longer sang as there was no more light of dawn. The night was permanent, the light had left the earth and it was a terrible place to exist. Pandemonium reigned throughout the world. The crime rate had escalated to widespread proportions. People were living in fear and many had lost all reason! Even I who had always been an eternal optimist and the glass three quarters full type of person, now mourned a world which lacked any lustre.

Those who held faith in whatever God they believed in prayed for hours each day in their churches, cathedrals, mosques and synagogues. The worlds' population either got down on their knees and prayed or sank into apathy. I dragged my enthusiasm for life back to the fore, then joined the rest of the congregation at St Roberts Catholic Church for an hour every day, lit many candles and made fervent promises to God if only he would return the world to its former glory.

On the 8th day after the forming of the black sky; the miracle finally occurred. The prayers and beseeching's of billions of human beings had finally been granted! If there were any doubts as to the existence of God they were dispelled that very day. The black mass of dense cloud started to dissipate like thick smoke from a chimney billowing slowly away, rising high up into the atmosphere until at last a hint of blue appeared once more. It was just a tiny speck at first but allowed a chink of light to filter through! At sight of this miracle the streets were crowded with people.

The mood increasingly changed from apathy to hopeful joy! It took many hours for the dense black mass of thick cloud cover to dissipate completely. Not one person who observed the transformations dared to feel complacent. Fear had been the constant companion of the world's population for what seemed an eternity! The inhabitants of the planet earth had grown accustomed to the oppressive blackness like a heavy cloak weighing them down into apathy!

At 6pm on that late July evening the sky was finally clear and once more was filled with vivid colours. It seemed to revel in bright and beautiful shades of blue, pink and violet. The sun appeared in the sky shining forth in all its former golden glory! The bright and glorious rays of sunshine touched the earth with its brilliant light and warmth. The world had once again transformed itself into a vivid pallet of fantastic shades of colour! The enigmatic beauty of the world was now fully restored to its natural state. The entire population of the world rejoiced at the miracle! Life was now once more full of hope and ready to be lived to the full!

Carla sat on a stool at the breakfast bar painting her long sharp nails deep blood red, in order to match perfectly the shade of lipstick she applied liberally to her lips every day. His step mother's cat like green eyes narrowed until they appeared as mere slits, and Kevin dreaded the way her gaze concentrated on him! He shuddered as a cold tremor ran along the length of his spine. The intensity of her stare, so cold it could freeze the rays of sunlight! Her hatred was tangible and he lived each day in fear of what Carla might be capable of!

'Who do you think you're looking at? Get on with your work Kevin or else you know what will happen! You really don't want me to have to punish you again!'

He carried on mopping the kitchen floor with renewed vigour determined to carry on cleaning until the tiles were pristine. He was well aware that she would experience a thrill from forcing him down the garden path to the shed; if the ceramic floor tiles were not spotless!

Why did dad have to marry her? It was a question he had asked himself a million times and still could not provide an answer. His dad never seemed to have any time to spend with him these days. It was Carla who commanded and received, all of his dad's attention. It seemed Richard was blind to anything beyond Carla's perfect face and nothing else mattered, he was totally besotted with her.

I reckon she is a witch, thought Kevin. She has put a spell on my dad! She looks just like a witch anyway! With her long straight hair black as ravens' wings, those intensely bright feline green eyes and the blood red lips. Almost everyone who met Carla agreed that she was an extremely beautiful woman. In Kevin's eyes Carla just looked scary! He knew from experience how thoroughly mean and nasty she was on the inside! When dad (or anyone else) was around she put on a perfect performance of being kind and considerate. Richard knew little of the woman with whom he shared his life. Carla's physical attractions held him dazzled and she allowed him only very fleeting glimpses of the woman he had married. She acted to perfection her starring role of loving wife and doting step-mother.

Kevin had tried unsuccessfully more than once, to speak to his dad about the way Carla treated him. Dad listened with half an ear then told his 12 year old son to stop telling lies, convinced the boy was inventing stories due to jealousy. Now he was almost certain that his step-mother had in fact used some kind of magic spell to get his dad to marry her. Carla finished painting her nails, screwed the lid back on the lacquer bottle then stepped off the stool leaving footprints on the damp floor tiles. Her green eyed gaze stared directly towards the anxious child!

'Look at the mess there are marks on the floor now you will have to start all over again. Just make sure this floor is spotless unless you want to spend some time in the shed!'

He cringed in fear at the thought of being locked inside the shed at the bottom of the garden. It was pitch black inside the old wooden building. The windows had been boarded up years ago, allowing not even a hint of light to filter through to the interior. The shed was filled with cobwebs complete with fat black spiders and numerous other creepy crawling insects lurking in the darkness ready to slither towards anyone who happened to be close by. Carla always checked his pockets thoroughly before she locked Kevin in the shed, making sure he had no matches, lighter, torch, or anything else which would allow him any form of light!

When Carla first set eyes on Richard that fateful evening in the exclusive club, she made a pact there and then to ensnare him. An extremely handsome man in his late thirties the epitome of the tall, dark, and handsome of numerous and varied romance fiction and countless films. His good looks were not the only attraction. She hadn't failed to notice him stepping out of his Silver Jaguar outside the club entrance.

There was no pastime Carla enjoyed more than spending money, preferably that belonging to other people. Sure enough like a cunning spider she weaved her silken web and within six months twin diamond studded wedding and engagement rings glittered on the third finger of her left hand.

The only fly in the ointment being young Kevin. He was so similar in looks to his mum with his chestnut wavy hair and extremely light blue eyes. Carla had no intention of competing with him for Richard's affection. She deeply resented the visible daily reminder of the late Mrs Stanford. Carla held an intense dislike for children, especially boys. She regarded them as noisy, totally abhorrent creatures, each and every single one of them. Kevin she reluctantly admitted had become extremely useful though it pained her to acknowledge the fact! He was becoming very proficient at his duties, namely cleaning the house and tending to the garden!

On their return from honeymoon, Carla gathered up every photo of Richard's late wife Sarah and removed them from sight. They were packed away in a cardboard box and placed in the attic. Kevin cried himself to sleep for many nights after this event. His grief over the loss of his mum was powerfully intense. Her love had always succeeded in allowing him to feel like the most important person in the world. Every time he attempted to talk to his dad about her, Carla would appear as if by magic! Richard never failed to be drawn towards her like a magnet to metal, or a fly being caught in the spiders' web.

It was just a couple of days since the floor mopping incident, when he'd repeated the task several times before she was finally satisfied the tiles were clean. Carla now complained that he hadn't polished the dining room table to her exacting standard and he would have to be punished.

Kevin felt the familiar dread well up inside him though it was not an entirely unexpected fact that this might happen. The difference being that on this occasion he was prepared. A stub of candle and some matches were placed inside a hankie and pushed down the front of his sweat shirt and lodged under his left arm out of sight. Carla searched his pockets then roughly grabbed his right arm and marched him out through the back door, hurried him down the path, unlocked the shed and pushed him roughly inside.

There was a strange expression on her face and her bright eyes glittered. Kevin thought she looked even more witch like than usual. He practically pleaded with her not to lock him in, otherwise her suspicion would have been aroused. She would have searched him more thoroughly. The door slammed shut, he heard the key turn in the lock followed by the click clacking of her retreating stiletto heels on the stone path.   As soon as it was quiet he lit the candle and dripped a little of the melted wax on to a saucer he found on the shelf. He placed the candle on the warm wax to fix it steady. This was the first time he'd had the chance to take a good look at the contents of the shed. Mostly it was just items of junk cluttering up the space. There were one or two things of interest though, for instance an old brass telescope and a model ship in a bottle. For the first time he hoped she would leave him in here for a long time. Pity he hadn't thought of a better hiding place for his candle and matches before today, but that didn't matter now. He shivered recalling the memory of all those terrifying hours locked in the pitch black darkness of the shed. His imagination running wild with the horror of what lurked close by. Carla would be extremely angry if she knew he was now unafraid, her own particular form of punishment was not going to make him suffer this time. He allowed himself a giggle, it was such a wonderful surprise! It was such a long time since he'd had anything to smile about and laughter was a thing of the long distant past!

'Kevin!'

He shot up from the floor at the sound of the urgent whisper in the dark!

'Who's there?'

This time a familiar, longed for, almost forgotten voice answered his question.

'Kevin I am over here my love.'

He shivered a moment at the shock of hearing her voice, then called out excitedly.

'Mum!! Where are you?'

He began frantically to search the shed, and soon found a large object leaning against the wall covered with a dust sheet. He nearly tripped over an old packing box in his haste to reach it. Carefully he pulled the sheet away to reveal a mirror set in a decorative gilded frame. Somehow it struck him that it might be ancient. Though this was just a feeling and he had no idea of how old it might be. Grabbing a bundle of rags he set about cleaning away thick dust and cobwebs from the surface. A few minutes later the silver backed glass was clear at last. He peered excitedly into the surface of the mirror. Kevin shuddered with fear and backed away in astonishment as a shadowy figure appeared in the crystal clear glass surface.

'Don't be afraid Kevin. It is me my love! Come closer let me see you.'

Slowly he made his way towards the mirror. The shadowy image inside the framed glass surface began to emerge ever clearer with each passing second. Tears suddenly sprang unbidden from the corners of his eyes and rolled down his cheeks blurring his vision. He roughly wiped them away with the cuff of his sweatshirt sleeve. Kevin looked at the mirror's surface once more and gazed in wonder at the image of his beloved mum. Her love for Kevin shone forth like a beacon from bright eyes: exactly matching the shade of light blue as his own. His heart now filled with so much love and longing he feared it would burst. He had missed her even more than he thought possible.

'Mum how? Why? What are you doing inside the mirror?'

'This mirror acts in a similar way to a television screen. You can see my image but it's just a projection right now. I have begged and pleaded with the powers that be for so long! Finally now as you can understand they have granted my wish. At long last I've been granted a brief period of time in order to help you my son. I love you so much Kevin and now have the means to stop that woman from ever causing you to suffer again. Now here is what I want you to do.....'

Kevin sat on the floor facing the mirror and listened intently while his mum outlined the details of her plan of action. Once Carla returned to the shed all he had to do was sit tight and wait! He was filled with the joy of sheer happiness. He'd forgotten how wonderful a sensation it could be. It was true that he hadn't experienced anything close to it since his mum was alive. They talked eagerly together for hours it seemed. She told him it was amazing to see how much he'd grown up over the last three years. She described in detail how wonderful it was and how much it meant to her to see him once again. Suddenly his mum abruptly ceased her conversation and placed a finger to her lips in a shushing gesture.

The loud click clack of high heels striking stones on the path outside had alerted both mum and son. Kevin spat on his hand and smeared his face in order to make it look as though he had been sobbing for hours. It was true that he had cried but the tears shed this time were those of pure joy at seeing his mum. The key turned in the lock, the door was flung wide open and Carla stepped inside the shed.

'I hope you enjoyed yourself Kevin!'

The words sour as lemon dripped spitefully from her cruel tongue.

'It's time for you to get back to work now. The shower room is in need of a thorough cleaning before Richard arrives home. We don't want him to think I can't look after the house, do we Kevin?'

She didn't expect an answer and giggled without even a hint of amusement. Her glittering green eyes devoid of emotion reminded him of a serpents. The mirror suddenly caught her eye the boy forgotten in that moment. She never could resist the temptation to admire and revel in her own beauty. As she gazed into the mirror her reflection confirmed what she already knew, that her looks were more striking than ever. She was transfixed by the sight of her own exquisite features. Her long black hair cascaded about her shoulders like curtains of silk. The crimson lips were soft and full. Her lips parted slightly to reveal teeth perfectly aligned, and even whiter than even she had ever noticed before.

Carla moved closer to the mirror, so entranced was she by her own perfectly exquisite beauty. Kevin was forgotten as she stared intently at the contours of her own face. The mirror shimmered without warning and the reflection became distorted. A blood curdling scream completely altered her features in an instant. A pair of soft white hands emerged from the silver backed glass of the mirror. The hands encircled Carla's wrists in a tight grip and pulled her inside the mirror. Her terrified screams were cut off abruptly as she fell forward and disappeared inside the mirror. Kevin observed in shock but his mother winked at him and beamed a smile of reassurance. He failed to see any of Carla's reflection inside the mirror and wondered what could possibly happen next.

Carla realised with mounting horror that she was now on the inside of the mirror as she gazed forward and spied Kevin sat facing it! She turned to face Sarah and the feeling of terror made her cry out in pure anguish!

'Why am I here? Where is this? How could you do this to me? You can't be here, you're dead. Help me! Please let me out.......'

Sarah shook the hysterical woman until eventually she remained still. The stream of endless pleading stopped abruptly leaving Carla silent but no less terror struck. Sarah loosened her grip and stepped away but held Carla rigid with fear in her steady blue eyed gaze.

'No more questions Carla you are here to listen! It is in your best interests to heed what I have to say right now; or face the consequences. Look into the mirror and you will see your true reflection. The mirror never lies, and the soul cannot hide your true nature!'

'No! No! No! That is not me!'

Kevin was no longer in sight, neither was the shed. The surface was now just another large mirror reflecting not her own beautiful features but an abomination! She screamed in horror and cried out at the terrifying nightmarish sight before her. The reflection in the mirror was the most grotesque creature she had ever laid eyes on. The thin haggard face of parchment like skin was covered in large weeping ugly red scabs and warts. The twisted pale red lips (like a gash in the ugly features) were drawn back to reveal blackened, jagged, teeth. The eyes black as a midnight sky, were hooded and without any lashes in order to attempt to mask the evil of their countenance. The hairs of the eye brows were bushy and unkempt. Long straggly strands of thinning greasy hair hung down failing to conceal a ravaged, deeply wrinkled neck. The screams of pure horror grew ever louder, until at last Carla's sheer terror became too much to bear, she crumpled visibly before collapsing to the floor. Hearing Sarah's voice she raised her head!

'Your soul is stained black to match that of your heart Carla. Ugliness is all you see in this mirror, because your true nature can't be concealed beneath the outer beauty. You are a mean spirited, heartless, malicious individual. My son has been forced to endure the brunt of your hatred and cruelty. Richard is totally infatuated by your beauty and foolishly believes every word you say! Eventually he will come to his senses one day but I can't wait any longer for that day to arrive.

I will set you free now but there is a stipulation that you have to abide by. It is an assurance that if ever you attempt to torment my son; the reflection you now see in this mirror will be yours for as long as you live. Your good looks are all that matters so you will have no qualms about agreeing to my terms and conditions.'

It was growing dark outside as the sun began to set, when Kevin eventually saw his mum appear standing behind Carla inside the ancient mirror. Carla looked completely petrified, and in some way very different to the woman who had been dragged inside its depths some time earlier. His mum face beaming in triumph smiled at him and winked in a conspiratorial manner. Kevin knew that whatever had taken place inside the mirror now changed everything .With both hands placed firmly on the other woman's back Sarah pushed Carla out of the mirror with such force she landed in an undignified heap on to the dirty floor of the shed. As Kevin gazed into the mirror his mum called out to him sounding already as if she were far away.

'I have to leave now my son but you will be just fine. Things are going to drastically change around here from now on. Carla is well aware what will become of her if she ever attempts to be cruel to you again so have no fear. I will always be watching over you. Goodbye Kevin, don't ever forget how much I love you.'

'Goodbye mum I love you too, so very much and thanks for coming. It was just so wonderful to see you again.'

His mum touched her lips to her hand then blew the kiss across the gap between them. For a fleeting moment he felt her warm lips touch his cheek one last time. Sarah stared into Carla's eyes with a look of resolve then faded from sight.

'Kevin please you have to forgive me I don't want to be ugly. I really will look after you and never treat you badly ever again. Your mum made me promise!'

He smiled with genuine happiness, things would be different from now on! No more scrubbing, polishing, or mopping floors for him. He ran down the path towards the house ready to enjoy life again thanks to his wonderful mum and the magic mirror of course!

Once upon a time long ago I became a living entity. Seeds were sown meticulously, into the deep dark fertile soil across several acres of farm land. The rich and varied nutrients in that fertile soil nurtured those seeds until they burst into life. They pushed forth green shoots through the dense earth reaching towards the sunlight. For many months the sun up above   and the earth beneath encouraged growth. Everything needed in order to gain strength and survive was provided by nature itself.

A trace of that life force survived after the hemp was harvested. After a lengthy process eventually the hemp was woven into thick coiled strands of rope. The first length of rope cut free from the strand became me, this was the first day of my existence!

Since I came into being many seasons have come and gone. The passage of so many years has taken its toll. In reality I have no concept of time passing by in terms of hours or even days. I am well aware though that a long period of time has passed since my first day. The years of hard toil have weakened my fibres considerably. There are frayed edges along the whole length and breadth of me. Little kinks have appeared which were not there before; causing weaknesses sapping the strength of me!

As an object I feel no discomfort from becoming older and weaker, but there is a semblance of awareness within. Each task undertaken throughout my existence, has left an indelible mark. Each and every one of the human beings I've been in contact with has left an impression on me. A miniscule semblance of their life force has been absorbed within my fibres. For me it is impossible to experience feelings like those of human beings or other living creatures. There can be no genuine emotion, but a form of memory is imprinted within my core.

My life has been both varied and useful. If the word life can be attributed to an object which has no heart; no soul; no feelings. Yet I do sustain a degree of perception if only by association with the contact of so many human beings.

I came into contact with the first human long ago, which left an imprint like a dark stain which can never be totally erased. On being cut into that first length of rope I was fashioned into a means of execution. This was the noose destined to be used for the death penalty. I found myself draped around the neck of a young man who was terrified of his forthcoming death. The quiver of his trembling body touched me with its unending terror until the trap door beneath sprang open. The jerking body violently quivering as the full length of my being (the hangman's rope) became reluctant executioner. That young man left his mark! Even though I have no emotion the impression of that horrific period of my existence is still as strong today as it was back then.

When the death penalty was finally abolished I was surplus to requirements and disposed of. No-one wanted to be associated with this particularly gruesome souvenir of the prison system. I lay in a field for a long while until a farmer found me and chopped off the noose end from the rope with a sharp axe. As the axe fell so I expected the dark stain to clear from my senses but this was not to be. Though emotion is not part of a rope's existence for some unfathomable reason there was a form of disappointment that it still remained a part of my being.

The farm became my home for many years. It was me the farmer used to tether animals, mainly horses while being led to and from the stables. A sense of the horses also left an impression within my core. I gained some insight into their very existence, just like people they also feel varied emotions, albeit on a very different level. As sentient beings they can suffer pain through illness or injury just as humans can. They can experience a certain kind of contentment. They also communicate on a level beyond the understanding of most human beings.

As time passed by the sheer daily toll of my workload became too much and I was badly damaged. The once brand new strong white fibres became grey and overstretched. I was not strong enough for that particular task at the farm anymore, which resulted in once again being discarded. I found myself lying in a patch of mud and leaves, half buried by the endless trample of human beings and animals, whose steps constantly made their way along the path through the woods. There is no inkling of how long I lay there!

One day a child spotted me lying there. He and another boy were running through the woods close to where I lay. His ankle became caught in brambles tripping him up to land on top of me. The two boys then moved the earth and leaves tugging with all their strength until I was freed. I was muddy and dirty but still some strength remained in my worn fibres. I was fashioned into a swing with a car tyre tied midway along my length and each end fastened to a thick strong tree branch. I became aware that the two boys were brothers and also best friends. The joy of their life as children unimpeded by responsibility left an impression which was immense. My time with them though positive failed to erase the black stain of my much earlier existence. The memory of the role I played out in the condemned block was vivid still. Being transformed into a swing was the kind of task which I found to be most worthwhile. If I were a human the only word used to describe that period of my existence would be 'contented'. As time passed by along a rolling wave of sunrises and sunsets, the seasons changed. Springs', summers', autumns', and winters' came and went as time marched on moving forward ceaselessly. The brothers grew up and went their separate ways. Once again I found myself discarded and alone.

Constantly I swung back and forth as the wind blew strong through so many season changes. On many occasions a person would wander along the path through the woods only to find me hanging from the tree. Mostly they would be tempted to sit in the tyre, to sway back and forth thinking their own private thoughts. Each time this occurred, a miniscule fragment of their essence imprinted itself into my core. In the main these impressions I absorbed were positive. Occasionally a boy or girl would swing back and forth for hours on end. The impressions sometimes gleaned were difficult to interpret, though I became conscious of still leading a useful existence.

One day I was cut from the tree and the tyre set free to be rolled away by a group of children. That tyre though attached to me for such a long time left no impression whatsoever. I lay on the ground beside the tree for a long, long time being soaked in the rain, and drying out in the sun growing weaker as the fibres were constantly stretched and shrank.

A group of young men walked the path through the woods one sunny day and found me lying on the ground. Once again I was retrieved from the dirt and made use of. The task I performed was very brief but also left a great impression in my core. The group put me to work in a tug of war competition at the local village fete. The combined essence of so many people coming in contact with me was quite overwhelming. That short stint turned out to be the last task I would perform. My useful existence had finally drawn to a close. I was unceremoniously thrown into a skip when the tug of war was won. I along with the other discarded contents from within the skip was transported to the local rubbish tip.

Over time the elements have taken their toll and I am no longer a full length of rope anymore. Bits of me have been cut off: shredded: burnt: scattered over the mound of accumulated rubbish. My sense of being still exists although in much more vague manner.

If I were a human being my soul would have departed from this earth by now. Human beings at the end of their lives will be buried under the rich dark earth for eternity. For me being buried in that dark earth is an experience I will relish.

I still retain that distant memory of bursting forth from that sown seed. The dark fertile soil rich with nutrients bestowed me with that vital strength needed to push forth through the dense earth. I remember the first contact with the sun. My stem rose up towards it gaining strength every day until fully grown. It may be the end of my useful existence! Objects just like humans and animals wear out over time and finally break down beyond repair. One day I will be reunited within that soil and finally allowed to rest as the memories are buried deep underneath the earth.

The Unknown Man

Somerton / Australia (1948)

Since the day I left my homeland, the process of change has been progressing in order to shield my real identity! The enunciation of my true origins has finally been meticulously discarded. I now speak with a flawless Australian accent. Each and every ex-citizen of German descent is naturally treated with suspicion, only three short years have passed since the end of the 2nd World War. In some instances the hatred of the German race is both palpable and without a doubt understandable. No-one is capable of understanding why it happened, nor can they forget the terrible crimes committed throughout the war by members of the Nazi party.

Throughout the years I have thought of little else beyond the need to track down the individual responsible for destroying my own family. I have dreamed of wreaking vengeance against the man whose actions were directly responsible in causing their deaths.

I live alone but never consider myself lonely. It's my own personal choice not to interact with others that much, and avoid them completely when possible. I travel to my place of employment and return home each evening having barely exchanged a word with another human being throughout the day. Every working day my routine is unchangeable.

At the weekends I also attempt to avoid any contact with people; unless of course it's absolutely necessary. Every Saturday morning I clean my tiny flat and tackle the laundry, then complete any other chores that need attending to. In the afternoon I shop for food, drink and other essentials. On Sundays I assemble the food and drink needed for a picnic, then head off to the beach. I make a point of deliberately choosing a place close to the rocks, and stay as far from other beach dwellers as possible. I like to swim in the sea and feel the surf flow over my body calming my soul. The water is both cleansing and refreshing at the same time. The beach is the only place I allow myself to indulge in the merest hint of pleasure. My life on the whole is an existence devoid of joy.

For a brief couple of hours I take pleasure in the cool blue green water, and revel in the warmth of the sun just like everyone else does, on the golden sun drenched sand. The minute I have packed up my things and begun to walk home, the pleasure of the water is quickly forgotten. The fleeting flame of joy is quickly extinguished to be replaced by the cold and oppressive weight of a vengeful soul. I am more automaton than human. I frequently dwell on the memory of those long ago days when life was both normal and in the main a contented one. I memorise the beloved faces of my family members which made life so worthwhile. For all the positive thoughts of the good times in the past, they do nothing to melt the band of ice around my heart. No action, nor indeed any person can possibly thaw the iciness that clings to my body and freezes the cold beating heart within.

This morning the day began in exactly the same way as any other usual Saturday. By the end of the day it would turn out to be far from ordinary! While waiting in the long queue at the bank this morning, suddenly I was aware of slivers of ice darting along the length of my spine. I turned my head slightly to the right and visibly shivered in pure shock on recognition of the familiar figure from my past. There in the next queue just a few short steps away from me, stood Maximillian Von Schtern! I fled the bank in a great hurry and waited outside, keeping partially concealed in a doorway.

Minutes dragged by as if they were hours while my heart rate quickened to an alarming speed. At long last he finally walked through the doors of the bank building and stepped on to the pavement just a few feet away, before walking along the main street. At a   discreet distance I followed his footsteps just close enough to keep him in sight.

I speculated on whether he could have the slightest awareness of being stalked. He turned his head quickly from left to right searching the crowds in a furtive manner. He walked briskly along the busy pavement but never once looked behind him.

At last he slowed to a stop before turning to the left and walking through the entrance of The Grand Somerton Hotel. I observed him through the glass doors as he headed to the reception desk and collected the key to a room. He stood by the lift entrance and pressed the button. The lift juddered to a halt and the sliding doors opened. As soon as he stepped inside the doors slid shut. I quickly made my way over to the reception desk.

'Excuse me miss. That man who just came in, could you give me his room number please?'

The young blonde receptionist gazed at me with suspicion in her eyes and for several seconds didn't say anything. Then she spoke in a voice that somehow tried to emulate a kind of authority and answered my question in a negative tone.

'I am not permitted to pass on any information regarding the guests.'

'No of course you're not. I wouldn't dream of asking, only he dropped his wallet in the bank. I tried to catch up with him and return it but he moved too fast.'

Her features relaxed a little as she smiled and provided me with the information.

'That is really very kind of you. In that case and under the circumstances I will make an exception. You will find Mr Goldstein in room number 28 on the 2nd floor.'

I thanked her for the information and headed for the lift. On reaching the 2nd floor a bell rang and the doors slid open. I stepped into the corridor and quickly glanced both left and right in order to make sure the coast was clear. I hastily wrote a message on the page of a small notepad that I always kept in the pocket of my jacket. I tore out the page and walked along the corridor to Von Schterns' room. I bent down and pushed the note under the door then quickly fled back to the lift. The doors opened immediately, thankfully I had not been seen. The corridor had been empty.

As I left the hotel my mind was in turmoil. What had brought Von Schtern to Somerton? How was it possible he had managed to track me down? Why would he even wish to find me? Right away I answered that question myself. Maybe I was the only person alive who knew everything about his past. It made me feel sick to my stomach that he was using a Jewish surname as an alias. How could he stoop to something so despicable? Not after all those terrible atrocities committed during the war.

In the past, Von Schtern was a member of and ran with a pack of hunters who tracked down their victims. Before the weekend was over he would come to understand the meaning of the word prey! Soon I reached the shelter of my home. Right away I retrieved the small leather case from its hiding place; inside the concealed compartment I'd created at the top of the wardrobe. I unlocked the case and checked the contents. Satisfied that everything I needed was tucked away neatly inside, I closed the lid secured the lock and pushed it out of sight beneath the bed.

For the remainder of the day memories poured, with such great speed and frequency into my brain I could barely think straight! My hands trembled at the thought of what tomorrow would bring. I was determined that my fear would not halt me in my quest for justice. Now that my purpose for living would soon be fulfilled. That heavy weight of guilt eased its burden on my slumped shoulders. I felt relief flood through me. I was content in the knowledge that soon the spirits of my long dead family, would be permitted to rest in peace. So many deaths! I have been haunted by the recollection of each one every single day of my life since fleeing the country of my birth.

At 5 o'clock the next morning my alarm clock rang out loud and roused me, though not from slumber! The previous night I had realised it was virtually impossible to close my eyes and drift down the path of longed for unconsciousness. I clutched the small case by the handle. My clenched palm clammy in the certain knowledge of who I was about to confront and the plan of action that would ensue. I closed the front door of the small flat behind me, knowing I would never return. There was no sentiment in the gesture, no looking back even though it had been my home for so many years.

The note I had pushed under the door of room number 28 on the 2nd floor of The Grand Somerton Hotel, contained the time and location of the meeting place; plus a short statement guaranteed to stir up the memories of the occupant. I had proffered not the slightest hint of information regarding my identity. He would definitely arrive on time, at the place arranged to meet of that I was certain. That he should also be armed with some form of weapon, was also guaranteed.

I arrived at the deserted beach 15 minutes early and concealed myself between a set of large jagged rocks well away from the main area popular with locals and visitors. I had the additional advantage of being in a good position in which to observe a wide area. More importantly I remained hidden from view. I reached into my pocket and retrieved my gloves. I pulled them on before unlocking the case and raising the lid. With the utmost caution I reached for the syringe already filled with the deadly toxin. Once injected the venom would cause almost instantaneous paralysis in order to prolong the suffering. Von Schtern was undeserving of any mercy and would receive none. The poison would quickly spread throughout his entire body shutting down the blood supply to all major organs; until at last the heart would finally stop beating and the brain would cease to function.

Minutes later I sensed rather than saw someone approaching. I peered carefully from my vantage point behind the rocks. Sure enough I could see Max striding along the beach. There was no mistaking the tall blonde haired figure who haunted my every waking moment. The handle of a gun in a leather shoulder holster was clearly visible, as the lapels of his jacket swung open. I would have to make my move fast. The adrenalin rush gave me the strength needed to propel me into action.

As Max approached the rocks I quickly moved through the gap behind me. Before he had time to react I lunged at his back catching him off guard. He tripped up, lost his balance and fell to the ground. I emptied the entire contents of the syringe into his neck. His body jerked in a convulsive motion. There was no opportunity for him to remove the gun from the holster, before the lethal toxin took immediate effect. His expression was a mixture of surprise and pure terror. I never imagined the effects of the toxin would be almost instantaneous, it came as a shock.

I crouched over his body and grasped his head in my hands then turned his face towards mine in order to see my eyes. Recognition was immediate and he tried to speak but made no sound. He managed to move his lips just enough to mime my name (Otto) before they stiffened in a grimace of abject fear and pain. I experienced no remorse whatsoever   that Max was dying a horrible death.

'I know that you can still hear me Max. You destroyed the lives of so many people throughout the war. I hoped and prayed that one day you would be caught, tried and convicted along with all the other war criminals. I read every single newspaper report about the trials at Nuremberg, but never gained the satisfaction of seeing your name among those caught and sentenced. It was an excellent job you did of disappearing without trace.

It was because of that our father committed suicide by blowing his brains out. Baron Heinrich Von Schtern was a true hero of the 1st World War, a highly decorated Luftwaffe pilot. How could he and our mother have contemplated that their own son would eventually be the one responsible for their deaths? Our own father could not bear the shame of knowing his son had joined the hated SS. When you progressed to becoming a guard at Auschwitz neither he nor our mother could bear the shame. The disgrace was too great, their hearts and spirits were broken.

I returned home from work one day soon after that to discover mother lying on the couch. At first glance I thought she was sleeping. I placed my hand on her shoulder and quickly pulled it away from her ice cold skin. My eyes flooded with hot tears and brimmed over streaming down my cheeks, to drip on the frozen mask like beautiful face of our dead mother. An empty pill bottle lay by her side. When our father came home from the university he found me still clinging to her corpse. His devastation was complete. The very next day he made arrangements to send me away. Some weeks later I received a letter from Aunt Gilda informing me that our father had committed suicide the day of mothers' funeral.

Now it's time for us both to die and very soon you will be in Hell. My life here on earth has been (Hell) for so many years it will be a relief to escape this world. '

His face may be a frozen mask but in his eyes I see a faint glimmer of life still burning. I am greatly relieved that he is finally paying the ultimate price for his many crimes against humanity.

I lift the lid of the small leather case once more and take out a piece of paper. Two words are written on it (Tamam Shud), which translates as (It is finished). Indeed those words are appropriate now my vengeance has been completed. I cut the labels from his clothing and make sure there is nothing left on the body which could lead to the identification of the corpse. It seems appropriate that he will be buried in an unmarked grave. Max is not worthy of the name Von Schtern. Once the body is placed in position against the rock I gaze into the eyes of my brother for the very last time. For the millionth time I wonder how; it could be possible that a member of my own family could have been responsible for such evil deeds.

Slowly I walk along the golden sands and into the beautiful blue green waters of the ocean. I revel in the refreshing feeling of surf on my face somehow cleansing the dark stain of my guilt. I swim away from the beach and head far out to sea. My arms and legs start to burn with the supreme effort of propelling my body onwards. I turn my gaze towards the sun and briefly take pleasure in the warmth of it on my face for the very last time. I dive down underneath the cool blue green waves edged in pristine white surf and allow my lungs to slowly fill with salt water. The long dead spirits of so many people can rest in peace at last. The great burden of avenging their deaths has finally been lifted. At long last I am more than willing to pay the price for taking one life by forfeiting my own. I sink beneath the water into oblivion.

I stood in front of the mirror taking a good look at my reflection. After no less than five changes of outfits finally I was satisfied with my appearance. Having joined the dating agency as a last resort I felt more than a little bit apprehensive. I had carried out extensive research beforehand to ensure it was reputable. As a detective in C.I.D it was the criminal element of society that kept those of us who were Police Officers fully employed.

It was the main reason I found it such a difficult task to meet any half decent sort of man to go out with. Apart from the unsociable hours due to my work commitments. As soon as my career in the Police Service was mentioned many people regarded me with suspicion. I had no intention of suddenly producing a warrant to search their premises, on the off chance they may be stashing drugs or stolen goods. That would be ridiculous but it didn't stop new acquaintances being a touch wary of me.

I was 27 years old and certainly not in the least bit hideous looking. My long wavy hair and sparkling green eyes had received compliments on numerous occasions. Despite my appearance and relative youth not one single man had asked me out on a date in the past two years. My career was going well and afforded me immense job satisfaction. Outside of work my personal life was really nothing to brag about. I barely socialised and needed (in fact change that to desperately wanted) that situation to change.

I glanced at my watch and noted it was time to go. The agency had set up a first meeting with someone named Steve. His photo revealed a friendly looking face, not exactly dream man material but he looked pleasing enough. I was more interested in personality than looks and hoped we would each find the other good company.

At 6.55pm I arrived at Marty's Restaurant five minutes earlier not wanting to appear too eager. But on the other hand neither did I wish to be late. One of my pet hates was bad time keeping. The waiter escorted me to a table and I ordered a drink hoping Steve wouldn't be long after all there was only five minutes spare in which to turn up. After sitting alone for a while not to mention attracting unwanted attention from the other diners, I was beginning to feel very uncomfortable indeed. It was 7.25 pm when it dawned on me Steve wasn't coming. The embarrassment of being stood up was escalated by the fact every single table at Marty's was filled with either couples or groups. I slowly sipped my glass of chardonnay and decided to order a Chicken Caesar Salad as the waiter was hovering close to my table. He was beginning to look most impatient!

I now studied the menu with such intent you would have thought it was a blockbusting thriller instead of a list of dishes. I ordered another large glass of wine and pretended that my own company were preferable to that of any dining companion. Inside the feeling of disappointment was depressing I silently cursed Steve for letting me down. The salad arrived just minutes later and I had to admit it looked delicious. The juicy chicken was char grilled to perfection with crisp fresh iceberg lettuce and very crispy croutons. I picked up my fork pushed it towards my plate ready to spear a piece of chicken when a voice called out.

'Please don't do that stop!'

The urgent tone of the voice was something I couldn't ignore but who was speaking to me. I turned my head to the left then to the right. The diners and waiters were all fully occupied with eating, talking, or serving customers. Again I lifted my fork eager to tuck in to the juicy looking chicken but before it reached my plate the voice called out once more.

'Please stop!!'

I stared all around me at the restaurants customers and staff. It was an odd sensation to hear a voice not knowing where it came from. Was someone playing games? Yet no-one seemed to look my way and despite the embarrassment of being stood up, it didn't affect my appetite I was really very hungry. I tried again to push my fork into a nice juicy piece of chicken when it suddenly darted across the plate. I only just stopped myself from yelling out in alarm. A sudden sense of apprehension caused me to remain silent. There was definitely something on my plate that had no place being there.

'Please take a closer look don't worry I am not an insect.'

The voice had an approachable tone so I took my reading glasses from the case and peered closely as a chicken piece moved slightly as something green appeared beneath a lettuce leaf. I gasped in sheer amazement as the something turned out to be a tiny man dressed in a dark green suit with a white shirt and a black tie. He couldn't have been more than a few centimetres in height. That wine must have been stronger than I thought! I blinked rapidly and glanced at my plate once more the tiny figure was still there. He spoke again and I was surprised at the strength of his voice for such a small figure.

'I realise you are wondering how it's possible to hear me so clearly.'

He pointed to the lapel of his jacket which held a tiny microphone and amplifier. I nodded to indicate my understanding. I was dumbstruck but stared at him with eyes wide open in wonder of the situation. He told me to eat a little as people were starting to stare. The last thing he wanted was to draw attention to my table or his presence. At long last I speared a piece of chicken with my fork and put it in my mouth it tasted delicious.

'First of all I need your help then you can ask me as many questions as you like later on. Can I count on you?'

'You can count on me I don't have any plans for the evening.'

'Thanks you look like the kind of person who does not shock easily. Maybe that has something to do with work please tell me what you do for a living?'

'I am a Detective Sergeant in C.I.D and as you say not much surprises me but then again you are the exception! Would you tell me your name?'

'As you can plainly see I am not a native of this planet so my name would be unpronounceable to human beings. I heard a waiter shout Joe earlier so you can call me that if you like.'

'Sounds fine by me I like the name Joe short and simple, pleased to meet you my name is Helen.'

I held out my finger to his tiny hand and he nodded and smiled in a conspiratorial kind of manner then replied.

'Very pleased to meet you Helen. If it is not too much trouble could you finish the meal and take me back to your home. Don't worry I am both honest and trustworthy!'

He laughed aloud the sound was so wonderful that I warmed to him right away. Pity he's not only tiny and green but also an alien; just my flipping luck, I thought. He may have a definite green tinge to his skin but there was definitely something about him. Secondly his sense of style was impeccable. His blonde hair was short and neat and his eyes were the most brilliant shade of green I had ever come across apart from my own of course. We had at least one thing in common even if it were only the colour of our eyes. I smiled on realisation of the way my thoughts were drifting. I blushed scarlet before laughing with embarrassment! It was just an impossible situation; an attraction between a mini alien and five feet 7inch human I have got be kidding!

I was suddenly aware that the voices in the restaurant had become very quiet, a quick glance around confirmed my suspicions. The other diners were all looking my way and their attention was the last thing I wanted. I carried on eating my meal until I came across a larger than average piece of lettuce! The fork in my hand hit a solid surface before moving away the salad and realising the object was not what it appeared to be! Joe called out!

'Helen please be careful that is my ship I need help to repair it can we leave now?'

I settled the bill and left a tip for the waiter. Then I opened my hand bag and carefully placed Joe in one almost empty compartment and the spaceship in another. It seems unbelievable that this situation appeared to me to be nothing out of the ordinary. My police training and experience had certainly paid off.

Once I arrived home my bag was placed carefully on a dining table. I removed Joe and the ship from the compartments then placed them with great care at the centre of the table. I went into the study, returning almost immediately with my magnifier on its stand. It was a present from my brother after he gave up his hobby of making miniature models. I positioned the ship underneath the lens. I was amazed by the exterior surface it was identical to a piece of lettuce. As I studied the ship in detail, Joe spoke a word of command

and the surface completely altered to take on the appearance of a scallop shell. He spoke again and the surface resembled a piece of marble. Yet another command and it turned to highly polished silver with a shape similar to a stealth plane. Joe spoke again and a hatch slid open to reveal the interior of the ship which was amazingly simplistic in design. That didn't mean   it was ordinary it was anything but I was awestruck!

'Joe your ship is just incredible if only there was a way I were small enough to go inside it and take a good look round!'

The two of us talked at great length and made plans for the repair of the ships' engine and damaged hull. I wrote a list of materials needed for the repairs which would be simple enough to get hold of. The following day after my shift ended, I managed to purchase every single item on the list. Never before had I been so eager to return home and relished the thought of helping Joe get started on the repair work. Joe adapted many of the items I brought home into miniature tools. He indicated the help I could give with some of the exterior repairs. We became great friends for such a mismatched couple and my fondness for him increased by the day. I began to dread the day his ship would be ready to fly off into the universe and ached with sadness knowing we would never set eyes on each other again.

Joe glanced up at Helen with a wistful look in his eyes. He would miss her more than she could ever imagine. What a wonderful woman she is, he thought. He never dreamed the science mission to earth would enable him to meet the lady of his dreams. He had thought of telling her that on his own planet the inhabitants were the same size as human beings. In order to penetrate earths' atmosphere, the molecular structure of both the ship and himself underwent a rapid change becoming significantly reduced in size.

Helen came home from work heavy of heart in the knowledge that today was the one she had dreaded coming over the past few weeks. Joe appeared to be both elated to be returning home to his planet but equally sad to be saying goodbye.

'Don't say it Joe. I know the ship is repaired and you have to leave!'

'I'll miss you so much Helen. Thanks for all your help. I will never forget you!'

He smiled and her heart took a jolt knowing that against all the odds she had fallen in love with him. It was going to take a long time to heal the heartache. Joe waived goodbye and entered the ship. A few seconds later Helen took the space ship out to the garden and placed it on the raised wooden bird table. The gentle buzz of the engine and the flashing neon lights of the ship were almost surreal! It rose straight up into the sky and disappeared from view in an instant.

Six months had passed since Joe left and Helen found she was unable to move forward. Her heart ached with longing to see him again. Her career was just as satisfactory, but regards to personal life it was empty. At home she was virtually a recluse. Her friend Sandy insisted she go on a blind date this evening and try to enjoy life. She glanced at her reflection in the mirror satisfied but hadn't made a great deal of effort. She was about to leave the house when there was a loud knocking on the back door. Odd to go round the back why not come to the front! She warily opened the door standing behind it in a defensive manner.

'Hello Helen I was wondering how you were fixed to help with a minor repair?'

The tall blonde haired man beamed a smile of pure joy. Her heart felt suddenly much lighter. His appearance was all so familiar except that his skin no longer had a green tinge and he was at least six feet tall! They clung to each other as their lips met in a passionate kiss. Then they moved apart to stare at each other in wonder before Helen finally answered his question.

'Hello Joe whatever needs repairing, there's no doubt I can help you fix it!'

Just for a second she felt bad about standing up the man she was to meet, but it was quickly forgotten. They stepped inside the house and she kicked the door shut behind them.